INSERTION
BOOK TWO OF MURPHY'S LAWLESS: MISSION CRITICAL

Chris Kennedy

Beyond Terra Press
Coinjock, NC

Chris Kennedy/Beyond Terra Press
1097 Waterlily Rd.
Coinjock, NC 27923
https://chriskennedypublishing.com/

Publisher's Note: This is a work of fiction. Names, characters, places, and incidents are a product of the author's imagination. Locales and public names are sometimes used for atmospheric purposes. Any resemblance to actual people, living or dead, or to businesses, companies, events, institutions, or locales is completely coincidental.

Edited by Charles E. Gannon.

Cover art and design by Thomas Peters.

Ordering Information:
Quantity sales. Special discounts are available on quantity purchases by corporations, associations, and others. For details, contact the "Special Sales Department" at the address above.

Insertion/Chris Kennedy -- 1st ed.
ISBN: 978-1648552427

This book is dedicated to the people who make things happen.

Chapter One

"Easy with it," Major Kevin Bowden said. "Easy...come right a little..."

The pilot, Burg Hrensku, initiated a ten degree angle of bank, keeping the laser from going into its gimbal stops. Bowden tweaked the joystick minutely, re-centering the crosshairs on the target—a guardhouse with two mounted .50 caliber machine guns. A second facility on the other side of the road was already a smoking ruin.

The crosshairs flashed, indicating the bomb had three seconds time of flight left, then the guardhouse detonated as the weapon struck home.

"Shadow, this is Hornet," Bowden transmitted. "The gates are down. I say again; the gates are down."

"Roger," the ground commander replied. "The gates are down. We are en route."

Two miles away, from behind a low hill, a column of vehicles started forward.

Bowden smiled and looked across the cockpit of the interface craft at his SpinDog pilot. "That's two for two. Looks like the drinks are on you."

"It is not fair," his pilot said. "With the new lasers and laser receivers your Colonel Murphy had us build, it is almost too easy."

"This one is, because no one's shooting at us. It gets harder when there are missiles in the air."

"Maybe next time I need to arm the indigs," Hrensku grumbled.

"Thanks, but no," Bowden replied. "I've been shot at enough for two lifetimes, thank you very much."

Bowden watched as the convoy proceeded past the wrecked guard posts and into the small village in the ravine behind it. Several muzzle flashes winked from inside the cluster of huts. The trucks stopped and the men inside deployed, going to ground to return fire.

The assault was over in ten minutes. The villagers had relied too much on the nested machine guns to keep them safe; they were unprepared for the new way of war the Lost Soldiers had brought to the planet. Bowden and Hrensku provided cover until the assault was over—they still had three more bombs if they'd been needed—then they returned to base.

Major Bo Moorefield was waiting for them as they came out of the debriefing room. "How'd it go?" he asked.

"No problems," Bowden replied. "The new tech works well, and the indigs weren't expecting their guardhouses to spontaneously combust. Looked like Cutter's guys didn't have much resistance."

"Good," Moorefield said with a nod. "Another one for the good guys." He cocked his head. "Hey, they're doing a quick turnaround on your jet." The interface craft—when they were used in an atmospheric role—had become "jets" over the last few months, even though the scramjet aircraft were definitely *not* like the jets the Lost Soldiers had left two hundred years and countless light-years behind them. "Murphy needs to talk to you upstairs."

"Ugh." Bowden shook his head. "Two RATOs in one day." The scramjets used rocket-assisted take off modules to get into the air for combat missions and trips to space to save fuel. Although the technology had improved recently, and they were less likely to malfunction, *less likely* didn't mean the modules didn't still fail spectacularly sometimes…making takeoffs far more dangerous than catapulting off an aircraft carrier, which Bowden had always thought was a crazy way to get into the air.

Bowden looked at Hrensku. "Want to take me upstairs?"

The SpinDog frowned, obviously not impressed with the idea of two RATO launches in a day, either, but then he sighed. "Sure. I need to get some of my stuff from the hab."

"Cool." Although Bowden was fully qualified to pilot the interface craft in the atmosphere, he wasn't qualified in space and needed someone to shuttle him up to the habitat.

"Let me grab a quick bite to eat," Hrensku added, "and then we can go."

"Would that work for Murphy?" Bowden asked.

"Yeah," Moorefield replied. "It was important, I think, but not urgent."

* * *

Several hours later, Bowden walked into the office of Colonel Rodger Murphy, the leader of the Lost Soldiers, aboard *Spin One*, the main rotational habitat of the Spin-Dogs.

"How'd the mission go?" Murphy asked after welcoming him.

"Good, sir," Bowden replied. "I'm getting pretty good at plinking targets with the new laser gear you got in the last download."

"Hopefully, there's someone else down there who can do it just as well as you, because I have something different for you."

Bowden arched an eyebrow. "Oh?"

"I can't give you all the details now, but I need you to learn how to fly spacecraft."

"Okay...can you at least tell me what types of ships?"

Murphy smiled apologetically. "All of them, at least for now."

"And that's all the info I get?"

"That's all you *need* at this moment. We're taking a look at some...opportunities we may have, and I want you prepared if they come to pass. Go. Learn how to fly as well—or better—in space than you do in atmosphere. That's a big enough task for now. I don't know how things are going to shake out, but I need you ready for anything."

Bowden shrugged. "I always wanted to be able to pilot the interface craft back up to the habs; I guess now I get to learn. I'm good with that, sir." He looked around the office. "Where am I going for this training?"

"The training will start here, probably move to Outpost for a bit, and then will come back here for the final bits."

"Okay..."

Murphy sighed and cocked his head, obviously trying to decide how much to tell Bowden. He gave a brief nod—just a single jerk of his head—to show he'd come to a decision and explained, "You will start by training with one of the RockHounds."

"Not one of the SpinDogs?"

"No, a RockHound. You probably haven't had much to do with them because they don't have much to do with R'Bak."

Bowden shrugged. "No, not a lot of contact, but I know they're scattered in small communities all over the outer system. Prospectors, miners, and salvage-monkeys, mostly."

Murphy nodded. "And because they spend all their time in space, they're the ones best able to teach you the tricks and traps of spaceflight. It was easier to have one come here to start the training since they don't really have 'cities' or big facilities to work out of.

"Once you generally know what you're doing, and your instructor pilot doesn't think you're too much of a hazard to people and equipment, he'll take you over to Outpost to run a few flights in a more austere environment. Once he's satisfied you can solo pilot in space, he'll bring you back here for the final portion of your training—flying to the planet and back. Since the RockHounds almost never go to the planet, a SpinDog will instruct you on that portion.

"Does it all make sense now?"

Bowden nodded and sat back in his seat. "Yes, sir, it does. When do I get started?"

Murphy looked over Bowden's shoulder and out the door. "Sergeant James, is Karas'tan out there yet?"

"Yes, sir," a voice replied.

"Please send him in."

A rather tall and thin man with dark hair strode into the room. The one thing Bowden noticed immediately was that the man's eyes never stopped moving for more than a brief second. *Search. Spot Target. Identify. Repeat.*

"This is Karas'tan Kamara," Murphy said. "He's the RockHound who will be teaching you spaceflight."

Bowden stood to shake the man's hand and met his scanning eyes. As they made contact, a corner of the man's lips dipped. Bowden chuckled to himself. *Already been measured and found wanting. Just like starting flight training in Pensacola all over again.* At least there weren't any drill sergeants yelling at him. Not yet, anyway.

"Good to meet you," Bowden said, suppressing a scowl of his own. "I'm looking forward to learning everything I can from you, although I'm sort of surprised to see you here."

"Why is that?"

"I would have thought we'd be meeting someplace, uh…"

"With less gravity? I've spent weeks preparing for the weight. It was not pleasant." He shrugged. "Are you ready to begin?" Kamara asked.

"Now?" Bowden said. The RockHound's lips—both corners this time—dipped again, and he looked like he'd just eaten something sour. Bowden smiled. "Of course, I'm ready. Let's go!"

The man nodded once, said his goodbye to Murphy, and led Bowden through the habitat to a small room with a table, a couple chairs, and a marker board.

"Most of our training will be behind the controls of a ship," Kamara said. "There are, however, a few things we need to cover before we get into one of the craft and begin flinging yourself around the system, as I'm sure you're in a hurry to do."

"Well, I hadn't really given it a lot of thought," Bowden replied. "My flight time has pretty much been limited to in-atmo work." He chuckled. "In fact, I didn't find out that I was learning spaceflight until about one minute before I met you."

"But your people have flown in space, yes? You are familiar, I hope, with the concepts of spaceflight?"

"Some," Bowden acknowledged. "I wanted to be an astronaut back when I first got into the Navy. I was on track for the program…but things happened that led me in another direction, then I wound up here, and I've pretty much been flying attack and support flights on the planet. There hasn't really been a lot of time to think about flying in space."

"What do your people do for this 'astronaut' training?"

"There's a bunch of classroom work, I know. Studying what craft you'll fly and space station systems—stuff like that—along with a bunch of other things like Earth sciences, meteorology, space science, and engineering. The astronauts in training also learn land and water survival, aircraft operations, and scuba diving."

"Scuba diving? What is that?"

"It's when you dive deep into a body of water and stay down for a long time using a rebreather or tank system."

Kamara's brows knit. "But your people *have* space flight, correct?"

"Yes."

"And you start out by diving in water?"

"Correct. Then the trainees—depending on whether they are going to be pilots or mission specialists—learn the different skills they need for their positions. Pilots learn to fly the craft and mission specialists to conduct spacewalks, perform robotics tasks, and conduct scientific research."

Kamara laughed for a few seconds. "That is *not* how we're going to do it here. We're going to skip the majority of that and go right into space. After all, we're here, and there are no bodies of water in which to do your scuba thing. Also, we will be flying small craft, especially to start. You will be a pilot and a *mission specialist* at the same time. There is no division of duties, beyond what I tell you. Every RockHound can fly *and* conduct spacewalks."

"You asked how we did it, so I told you," Bowden said. "I'm prepared to learn the way you want to teach."

"Are you?"

"Am I what?"

"Are you really prepared to learn? Your people show up here and immediately change the way everything is done. We have been safe here for many centuries, yet now we are exposed because of your blundering. Then, afterward, you start telling us how things are now going to be done, and why we have to do it 'your way.'

"I have trained a number of SpinDogs in spaceflight, and the ones who have had the hardest times are those who were already familiar with flying in atmosphere. Spaceflight is different. Just because something works in atmosphere doesn't mean it works the same way here."

"Look," Bowden said. "You can tell me everything you want—everything you can, really—about how to fly in space. I'll gladly learn at your knee. It's my understanding, though, that you don't fly in atmosphere, so don't knock my piloting skills until you can land a plane on a ship. When you've done that, *then* we can talk."

His eyes got wide. "You've landed aircraft on ships? Like, the kind that operate on water? On purpose?"

"Yeah. Of course, the ships were a little bigger than the largest ones I've seen on R'Bak, and the aircraft were smaller than the interface craft I've been flying, but the principle is the same. Big ocean, little ship, and land the plane on it."

"In a hover, like I've heard your helicopters do?"

"No, landing on it like an aircraft does at the airfield. Except the airfield is on the water, moving in all three axes, and is a whole lot shorter."

"I don't think I'd want to do that." Kamara's eyes narrowed. "It would seem to take a certain kind of suicidal idiot to even attempt it."

Bowden chuckled. "Yeah, that's what we thought sometimes, too." He smiled. "Regardless, I've done that, and you haven't, so how about giving me at least a little respect for my piloting skills, all right?"

A smile ghosted across Kamara's face, then he gave a small twitch of a nod. "If you have rendezvoused with objects moving in all three axes, perhaps you will manage to earn my respect. I will tell you again, though, the people who have the hardest time with space-flight are the ones who have a lot of atmospheric flight time."

* * *

"This is what we'll be flying," Kamara said later as they approached a small packet-type craft in one of the habitat's docking bays.

"Really?" Bowden asked. "Doesn't look like much." He'd seen some of the smaller craft before but hadn't paid them much attention. They were fairly spindly-looking compared with in-atmo craft. "Where'd you get it from?"

Kamara frowned. "That's my ship."

Oops. Open mouth; insert foot. "Sorry," Bowden said. "I didn't mean anything bad by that. I just assumed you'd need something bigger, for umm…exploring things and bringing back ore and…" He tried to come up with something else to add but couldn't. He tried a different tack. "I expected we'd be flying one of the interface craft, since I'll have to learn liftoffs and re-entries with it."

Kamara shrugged, looking away. From his tone, Bowden could tell he was only partially mollified. "Perhaps if we had your capabilities, where we could destroy anyone who wasn't our friends in the system, we might use bigger craft that are more noticeable. Then we also could fly wherever we wanted, whenever we wanted. As it is, though, we stay alive by staying hidden, and this craft is a lot easier to hide than the SpinDogs' interface craft."

"That makes sense," Bowden said. He chuckled ruefully. "With our friends no longer here in the system, it's probably a skill I need to learn, too. Maybe even more so than launches and re-entries. Getting caught by a Kulsian military craft wouldn't have a very good ending."

"It would not." Kamara shrugged. "Besides, this craft is a lot better for prospecting. It's more maneuverable, which also makes it a better ship for you to learn on. There's less chance of you wrecking it. It's also smaller and less expensive so it will be cheaper to fix when you do ultimately wreck it."

"I thought that we already agreed I had flying skills."

"No, we agreed you had flying skills in atmosphere. *You* agreed that those skills translated into skills that were applicable to flying my ship. They are not. Almost everyone crashes spacecraft when they are learning, especially pilots with any significant in-atmo experience. Things don't work the same in space, and your eye—the way you view things—is going to tell you things that will be untrue in your new environment."

"Like what?"

"We'll get to that, but for the moment, you'll have to take it on faith." Kamara shrugged. "Let me show you the ship." He led Bowden around the craft, showing him the various systems. As a

Navy Test Pilot School graduate and an applicant for the astronaut program, Bowden was able to understand the systems, even the ones he hadn't necessarily seen before, like the asteroid capture system.

As they went around, a new question formed as he looked at the systems bolted to the skin of the packet. While some looked to be permanent fixtures, others were obviously new and didn't look like a lot of thought had been put into where—or how—to hang them. "Are all these type of craft the same?" he finally asked.

"No," Kamara replied. "The main parts are generally inter-changeable—motors, fuel tanks, and such—but every RockHound has his or her own needs. Where they're going, what they're doing, and how they're going to do it once they get there. About the only thing in common is that you won't see any that are appreciably big-ger than this ship."

"Because of the need to hide?"

Kamara nodded. "Exactly."

They started down the starboard side, and Bowden chuckled.

"What is it?" Kamara asked, sounding defensive.

"It's nothing." He pointed to a laser range finder. "If nothing else, I have experience with *that*. It's what we use to bomb with." He smiled. "It looks a lot better on your ship than the way they first wired it into the interface craft."

Kamara looked around the hangar bay. "Don't ever trust a Spin-Dog to wire anything into your craft. They are—" he thought for a moment, "—sloppy."

"What do you mean?"

"They don't work on craft as if their lives depended on their re-pairs. Sure, *they do*...but they never go very far from the habitats or the Outpost. Somebody can always go retrieve them if necessary. We

go out on our ships for months, prospecting and salvaging, harvesting oxygen and hydrogen from ice, and we are often out of range of
help. If you are two days away from the nearest ship or ice chunk
and find out you have a day's worth of air remaining because there
was a small leak…" His voice trailed off ominously.

"Yeah, that would be a bad place to be," Bowden agreed with a
nod. "Got it; always check everything that's been done to your craft
when someone else has been working on it."

Kamara nodded seriously. "You should always treat everything in
this ship as if your life depended on it. It does."

Bowden took a deep breath and nodded. It wasn't something
he'd really considered before. Sure, you preflight your aircraft before
you accept it and take it airborne, but it was easy to dismiss small
leaks or other minor problems. He'd once pointed out a puddle of
hydraulic fluid under the aircraft next to his on the flight deck of the
aircraft carrier. The Intruder guy had laughed and said that was normal. "If it ain't leaking, you better get it serviced 'cause it's empty,"
the bombardier had said at the time. Taking a ship into deep space
for months at a time, though, would require a whole new level of
detailed preflight.

You can't just eject out of a spacecraft if it stops working on you.

Kamara chuckled. "I can see from the look on your face you
grasp the seriousness of knowing your systems are operational."

"Yeah. It's not a matter of life or death. It's more important than
that."

"It is," Kamara said.

"Do you have the tac manuals for the equipment?"

"'Tac manuals?'"

"Yeah, the publications that tell you how to use the equipment. I'd like to study them before we get started. Learn the checklists."

"We do not have tac manuals. That is for SpinDogs. Some of the equipment comes with an installation or operating guide, but most do not. And we do not use checklists. Everything is too individualized with each craft. There is no standardization; you just learn what your craft needs and do it."

"How about a wiring guide so I know how things are powered?"

"Did I not say that most ships are individualized? The wiring will vary with the ship and how it's used. Not to mention everyone's ships have different electrical busses..."

"How do you learn all the systems, then, if you don't have the system specs for your gear?"

"You learn from one of the existing shipmasters." Kamara winked. "And you're one of the luckiest people on this hab."

"Why's that?"

"You've got *me* to show you not only the ship itself but also how to fly it." He smiled. "Let's step inside, and I will show you the interior."

* * * * *

Chapter Two

"Your controls," Kamara said three weeks later as he took his hands off the stick. He looked over and smiled.

Bowden forced himself not to wipe at the sweat pooling on his forehead as he took control of the spacecraft. Kamara had already shown him the intercept twice, and he'd made it look ridiculously simple both times. Before Bowden could even see what Kamara was doing, they'd been alongside the target, close enough to grab it with the packet's claw arm.

Bowden nodded once as he found the target outside the canopy. *All right, here's where you shut this bastard up by performing the best rendezvous you've ever flown.* He oriented the small craft with a puff of the control thruster, then another to null out the first one's thrust once he had the craft aligned the way he wanted. Bowden thrusted toward the target: a pod from a small rotational habitat the Dornaani had wrecked as they bulled their way through the system. Bowden kept a close eye on the target and gave two bursts from his thrusters, but—despite the thrust he'd given the packet—the pod seemed to move away from him and downward.

Bowden took a deep breath and released it slowly. *I've got this.* He lost sight of the target and pitched the spacecraft's nose down to find it again. As it came back into view, it now seemed to be traveling on a different track from what it had been, and he frowned at it in concentration. *You're not getting away that easily.* Satisfied with the orientation, he again thrusted toward it. The pod—as if it had a mind of its own—again moved away from him and down. He tried the rendezvous a third time, but never got any closer than he had on the first run. All he succeeded in doing was moving higher and farther away.

"*Damnit!*" he exclaimed as it drifted off again.

He looked over to find Kamara chuckling. "I've got the controls," the RockHound said.

Bowden gratefully relinquished control of the craft, and his shoulders slumped. Before he could clear his head, the pod filled the front canopy, close enough to touch, its trajectory matched perfectly by the small packet.

"Okay, damn it, how did you do that? The more I drove toward it, the further it moved away."

"It's all a matter of understanding orbital mechanics. The pod isn't moving away from us; you're taking us away from it."

"How so?"

"It's a matter of energy. You looked out the canopy at the pod, then you aimed and thrusted hard toward it. However, by giving the craft more power, you caused it to fly faster which moved you higher in orbit."

Bowden looked out the canopy at the large moon below him, which orbited the fifth planet in the system, and shook his head, trying to understand.

"As you moved to a higher orbit," Kamara continued, "the pod seemed to fall away from you, but it was an optical illusion; it stayed in its same orbit and you moved away from it. Although it seems counter-intuitive to your eyes, which are used to flying in atmosphere, you needed to slow down to catch up to it."

Bowden thought about that a little and held up his hands to simulate the two craft and how the rendezvous was supposed to occur. Finally, he shook his head. "Okay, I can see what you're saying, and I guess it makes sense. Faster pushes you out to a higher orbit. What I don't understand, though, is *how the hell you make rendezvousing with the pod look so damn easy!*"

Kamara's smile grew. "Practice, mostly," he said. He tapped the controls a few times, changed the packet's orientation, and the pod appeared again in the cockpit window, about a hundred meters away.

"The way you do it," Kamara said, "is that you have to visualize it backward. Instead of looking at the target and driving toward it, like you would in the atmosphere, what you really have to do is visualize the intercept point and work backward from it. The pod is in orbit, and we want to get the ship to it, so where do you have to put the ship so that as you slow down or speed up—either will work—the pod gets closer, and we meet it at the spot you visualized?"

Kamara cocked his head. "Does that make sense?"

"I think so…in some sort of twisted, bizarre logic. Basically what I need to do is not look at the target so much as fly the craft to where we intercept the target's orbit."

"Exactly," Kamara said, smiling. "Nothing could be easier."

Punching you in your self-satisfied face would be a hell of a lot easier, actually, Bowden thought, but instead he said, "Do I get another shot at it?"

"One more," Kamara said, looking at their plot. "It's going to burn a lot of fuel to get the pod back to the habitat from here."

"Fine."

"You've got the controls."

"I've got 'em," Bowden replied. *Just don't fuck this up. Just don't fuck this up. Just don't fuck this up.*

Understanding the concept, Bowden found, wasn't the same as understanding the course of action necessary to bring about the desired action, but at least he now understood the issue well enough to not approach the solution backward. Pursing his lips, he visualized where he wanted to meet up with the pod and applied a touch of the thruster that would slow him.

Nothing seemed to happen. It might have moved a little closer, but it was hard to tell. He goosed the thruster a bunch harder.

"Easy," Kamara said as the pod grew larger, quickly. "Going easier on the thrusters and being more patient will make things—shit!"

Bowden had tried to take out some of the closing velocity by hitting the retro thrusters; however, he had changed the orientation of the rendezvous, and the imparted energy drove them faster toward the orbiting pod.

"My controls!" Kamara yelled. He grabbed the stick and initiated a full burn.

Slam! Metal screamed and tore as the ship glanced off the pod.

"Put your helmet on!" Kamara said urgently. He got the ship under control, then he fastened his own helmet.

"Are we losing air?" Bowden asked.

"I don't think so. But it's always a good precaution to put your helmet back on until you're sure you're not. A slow leak is insidious. You feel yourself getting warm and happy as you asphyxiate, and then…nothing."

"So what do we do now?"

"We go back to the habitat and assess the damage."

"Without capturing the pod?"

"Yes, without capturing the pod. Hopefully, we didn't knock it out of orbit enough that it will re-enter and burn up. There was probably a bunch of good stuff onboard, besides what I would have gotten for the pod itself."

Bowden winced. "Sorry."

Kamara shrugged. "It was my fault for trusting too much in your skills. Hopefully, we can go back after it tomorrow. If the ship isn't too badly damaged."

Ouch. Nothing like a mid-air collision on your first familiarization flight.

* * *

They flew the rest of the way to the habitat in silence, and Bowden could tell the RockHound was worried about the damage he'd done to the ship.

They landed, and Kamara shut down the ship and was out of his seat before Bowden could grab his stuff. Bowden found him looking at the bow of the ship, where three deep gouges ran for about four feet across the nose. A couple of wires also protruded from where something used to be mounted.

"Sorry," Bowden said. He pointed. "What used to be there?"

Kamara scoffed. "Auxiliary rangefinder."

"Why didn't we use it?" Bowden cocked his head. "Wait a minute, when we were going through the list of gear, you said your ship had a computer that let you calculate intercepts. I know it was rudimentary, but why weren't we using that?"

"Because technology breaks." Kamara shrugged. "And sometimes it leads you astray. It can't be trusted. You have to be able to do intercepts visually, so that you know when the technology is wrong. There might be times, like in an emergency, where you'd have to use it, but I would never actually want to *have* to use it."

Bowden chuckled.

"You think that is funny?" Kamara asked.

"No, not really, but when you first showed me this craft, you told me I was going to wreck it."

Kamara raised an eyebrow. "And?"

"At the time, I would have bet you that you were wrong."

Kamara waved toward the craft's nose. "It appears you would have lost."

"Yes, I would have."

Kamara looked at him for several seconds. "So?" he finally asked.

"So, I'm trying to work my way around to saying I'm sorry, but pilots have a hard time saying negative things about their skills in the first place, and then admitting they were wrong in the second."

"And?"

Bowden took a deep breath and let it out slowly. "And you were right. I was wrong. My in-atmo skills didn't translate into flying in space. And I *did* wreck your craft."

Kamara smiled warmly, the first time he'd done so. "Good. Now that you have admitted that, perhaps you will actually come to believe it, and then we can *really* make some progress."

Bowden gave him a half smile. "I do believe it. And I hate that Murphy is going to take the cost of repairs out of my paycheck. Well, we don't actually get a paycheck at the moment, but I'm sure it's going to cost me somehow."

Kamara shrugged. "The damage isn't that bad. I'm not sure we'll even need to mention it to your Murphy."

"No? You think those gouges will buff out?"

"I do not understand. 'Buff out?'"

Bowden explained the concept.

"Ah," Kamara said with a chuckle. "We would say, fill with dust." He shook his head. "I said it wasn't that bad, but it *will* need to be fixed before we can take it out again. And we'll want the range-finder. One of the maintenance people here owes me a favor, though, and perhaps we can do him a favor the next time we go to Outpost. If you're willing to assist him in mounting the module—"

"I am," Bowden interjected with a nod.

"—then he probably won't charge us, and there'd be no reason to have to mention it to anyone."

"That's great."

"No, what would be great is if you were willing to listen to me."

"I am."

"Good, then let's talk about inertia while we wait for my friend to come on duty."

* * * * *

Chapter Three

"That's it?" Bowden asked a month later after he'd finally learned how to do orbital rendezvous, and they'd moved on to the next stage in his training syllabus.

"Yes, that is Outpost."

"Shit," Bowden muttered. *Game time.*

Outpost was an oblong asteroid, just like the habitats. However, where the spins revolved around their long axes, like logs rolling in a pond, the eight-hundred-meter-long Outpost rotated end over end, tumbling along in its orbit. Located thirty million kilometers behind the cluster of rocks in R'Bak's spinward Lagrange point, the asteroid tumbled in a very "clean" spin—there was no roll or yaw to upset the centripetally-generated "Gs" that existed at the ends of the rock.

"I will take it in the first time," Kamara said after they had spoken with the station and gotten clearance to approach, "so watch and learn."

I learned so much watching him rendezvous with the pod, Bowden thought with a small sigh. *Hopefully, I can do better this time.*

"Okay," Kamara said. "What do we know about inertia?"

"Objects travel in a straight line unless a force acts on them to make them stop or change."

"And why do we care?"

"Because any force that I impart to the craft will require a nulling force. I won't automatically start slowing once I let off the throttles, like I do in atmosphere."

27

Kamara nodded. "It is far better to go slowly and be patient. If you hit the thrusters hard like you did when we were first at the pod, you had better be using them to break away from Outpost, rather than trying to recover from a shitty approach. If it looks like the rendezvous is going badly, break it off. As you said before—"

"Easy does it," Bowden chorused with him.

"And, what's the most important thing about flying near Outpost?"

"Don't fly through the railgun launcher's firing path."

"Not just 'don't fly through its launch path,' but understand—and be aware of—where it is at all times. Other ships will be maneuvering to avoid it, and you need to watch for their movements, too."

Kamara's words proved prescient; as they approached Outpost, the railgun mounted in the center of the asteroid fired, launching a payload tub in the direction of *Spin One*. Bowden had shaken his head when the launcher had been explained to him; it was a massive railgun that was used for launching very small craft and drones from the station, as well as to send material—and, rarely, people—between Outpost and the habitats. The tubs weren't much larger than a person and required the receiving end to capture and bring the tub aboard the habitat. If they missed or forgot—or a thousand other failures—the person went flying past the habitat, heading out-system. It was a transfer method that wasn't used for people very often due to the dangers involved and the fact that they'd have to endure a five-second acceleration at over ten Gs. Or thereabouts.

And one I am never *getting in,* Bowden thought as the tub flew past their craft.

Bowden watched as Kamara flew the packet past the launch path and then around to land on the asteroid; Bowden kept his hands above the controls, going through the motions as if landing the craft himself. He'd gotten better at rendezvousing with objects in space in the four weeks since he'd ripped the rangefinder off the nose of the craft. They'd gone back for the pod the next day and had actually found the device; it was imbedded in the pod. Unfortunately, it was smashed beyond use and had been turned in at Spin One as scrap/salvage, along with the rest of the salvage they'd obtained from the pod.

Kamara refused to use the craft's navigation system to assist with the approach, even though Kamara had told Bowden he was satisfied the Lost Soldier could perform a rendezvous manually. The nav system might have been helpful with this approach—Bowden had no way to know, since he hadn't used it—because the big asteroid was tumbling along at a rate of seventy seconds per revolution, so they needed to arrive at the precise location at exactly the instant necessary to capture the asteroid's docking collar. And at the matching radial velocity.

Bowden risked a quick glance over to his instructor. Although Kamara had said the approach was "no big thing," Bowden could see the intense concentration in the RockHound's eyes and the faint sheen of sweat on his forehead. It was obviously a much more difficult evolution than Kamara had let on.

Unlike chasing objects in orbit, there were some obvious parallels between this approach and landing an aircraft on the aircraft carrier. You were trying to meet an object at a certain point on its surface while it moved through three dimensions. There were plenty of differences, but the approach itself was straightforward in nature.

The one thing he noticed as Kamara flew the craft inbound was the way the RockHound kept a light touch on the thrusters. When landing on the aircraft carrier, the pilot flew a specific glideslope, which he referenced by keeping "the ball" centered between two reference datums. When the ball went high, you reduced power to bring your glideslope down; you added power when you were below glideslope to get back on it. The trick was to smoothly intercept the desired position and not go from a low to a high back to a low again. That was called "chasing the ball," and ended up with the pilot using increasingly larger throttle adjustments as he got in close. Bad juju.

Kamara, by keeping the thruster adjustments small, was able to keep the craft at the right velocity to arrive when the docking collar was in position to receive them.

Not sure I'm ready for this, Bowden thought as the locks clicked and the motion of the packet changed drastically as it took on the spin of the asteroid, with all the subtlety of a medium-velocity car crash. While he understood getting the right velocity to arrive when needed, there was also the side-to-side thrusters he needed to manage, as well as the up-and-down velocity needed to drop into the docking cradle in that incredibly short interval where you were in position to do so.

"Nothing to it," Kamara said, sitting back in his chair. Judging from his reaction, though, it was obviously not something even the experienced RockHound found "easy."

"Yeah, right," Bowden muttered.

"Do you need a break before you try it?"

"No," Bowden replied. "And there is no try."

"What?"

Bowden's voice took on an ominous tone. "Try not. Do, or do not. There is no try."

He looked over at Kamara, whose brows were knitting. "What are you talking about?" the RockHound asked.

"It's from...never mind. Too hard to explain. Yes, I'm ready." He took a deep breath and let it out heavily. "Let's do this."

Kamara touched the controls then made a show of taking his hands off them. "Your controls."

Bowden nodded. "I have the controls."

"As soon as you release from the docking collar, give the thrusters a boost away from the asteroid before you do anything else," Kamara instructed. "There are some bulges on it that stick out a little further than where the collar is, and we don't want to have them hit us."

"No we don't," Bowden replied. He went over his new mantra as he thought through what he needed to do. *No more mid-airs. No more mid-airs. No more mid-airs.*

"Okay," Bowden said. "I'm ready."

"Very well, take us out a hundred meters from the asteroid."

Bowden nodded, then realized the motion was probably lost inside his helmet. "Got it." He released the docking collar clamps then gave a gentle boost away from the asteroid. The ship slid away from Outpost, its orbital motion different from the centripetal force it had imparted to the packet as Bowden let go of the clamps. He then took the craft away from the asteroid, careful to avoid the railgun launch path. There were no more launches scheduled, but, as Kamara had taught him, if you never flew through the launch path, you'd never get hit by something being shot out of the tube.

Kind of like walking beneath bombs hanging from the wings of aircraft on the flight deck—they will never fall on you if you don't walk under them.

He pushed that thought aside as he stabilized the craft in a position one hundred meters out from the asteroid and concentrated on finding the rhythm of the big rock's tumble. After a couple of revolutions, he realized it was like trying to time the waves in the ocean when you were about to run out into the water. *Except you could always dive into a wave if you miscalculated.*

"Any time you're ready," Kamara said as the rock began its third revolution.

"Next time around," Bowden muttered. He thought—but didn't add—*you asshole.*

As the docking collar reached the "bottom" of its tumble, Bowden nudged the craft forward. As the asteroid rotated, though, he realized his boost was going to get him to the asteroid before the collar was at the "top" where he could latch onto it. He gave the thrusters a little tap to slow the craft, careful not to "chase the ball." *Small adjustments over a longer time period are better than big power variations you have to null out.*

"Shit," he muttered as the craft started to drift to the left. He tapped the appropriate thruster, then tapped the opposite one to null the thrust. The craft still had a little velocity in the correct direction to bring them back into alignment, but he'd have to null that before capture.

In the Hornet, his scan on approach was "meatball, lineup, angle of attack," and he tried to work out something similar. After a few seconds, he settled on checking the arrival position of the asteroid and his lineup out the cockpit window, then checking the craft's velocities inside on the gauges.

As the ship reached the correct lineup, he nulled the drift, with a glance inside the cockpit to check the velocity. It showed him overcorrecting. He put in a correction for it. His eyes went outside the craft. *Damn that thing is big and close!* He fought the urge to shy away from it as the close end of the asteroid rose toward him. It looked like it was going to slam into his craft, but it was the same sight picture as when Kamara had done it—he wasn't screaming about their impending crash, either, which was a good sign—and Bowden knew he had to be close enough to grab the collar. If he shied away, he wouldn't be able to get back into position in time.

The ship slid to the left and he gave it a boost back to the right. Too hard. He tried to catch the momentum, but it overshot the collar as it rotated into alignment. He tried to boost the ship back into position for a second dive at it but clanked off the side of the collar as he went past. Kamara slapped the thrusters, hard, to boost away from the asteroid.

"What the hell?" Bowden asked.

"You were about to crash into the asteroid. I boosted us up and away from it." He paused and then added, "Get away from it and look at the tapes."

Bowden sighed and flew the craft back to the pre-approach position, then he watched the tapes of the approach while Kamara piloted the craft. Everything was good until he got in close, then he overcorrected several times and made a big play to capture the docking collar. He winced. Kamara was right. He probably *would* have hit the asteroid if the RockHound hadn't boosted them away.

"You're right," Bowden said with a sigh. "As always."

"Of course I am," Kamara acknowledged with a smile. "What I want to know is, what happened? You had a nice approach going, then lost it—badly—at the end."

"I thought I saw a drift on the range-finding system. I overcorrected a couple of times, then made a play to grab the collar."

"When you saw the drift on the system, did you see the same thing visually?"

"Well, no. The lineup *looked* good."

Kamara shrugged. "Sometimes the range-finder gets spurious inputs in close due to vagaries of the asteroid's surface and its spin. You know what doesn't get bogus inputs?"

"No, what?"

"Your eyes. If you look out and you're not drifting, *then you're not drifting.* There is a science to flying in space, but there is also an art to doing it well, too. You have to use your feelings and believe in what you *know* to be true."

"Go with your gut?"

"What does that mean?"

"It means I have to use my instincts."

Kamara nodded. "Exactly so." He shrugged. "Besides, you can't count on technology. If you become reliant on it, you are crippled when it doesn't work."

"Which is why you had me learn to rendezvous with objects in orbit without using the system."

Kamara nodded.

"So, why didn't you have me do this without using any of the technology, too?"

"This is different. There are more variables, and the chances of smashing the craft—as you showed—are a lot higher. I didn't want to destroy the ship and get stranded here."

Bowden thought about what Kamara said for a few seconds then shook his head. "I'm sorry, but I really don't see how this is any different. We're rendezvousing with an object, same as we were in orbit, but, this time, we don't have to fight the orbital mechanics as much. Sure, they're still there, but the effects are smaller. And if I hadn't fallen for an erroneous system indication—"

"You did fall for it, though," Kamara interrupted.

"I did, but I shouldn't have," Bowden said. "It's just a matter of learning the right things to watch and when to watch them." He shrugged. "There's also a different set of flight controls I'm still getting used to, too, which complicates things a little, but the better I get with the controls, the better I'll be able to rendezvous with things. Not having to actively search for where the controls are would give me more time to watch what I need to watch."

"That is true."

Bowden took a deep breath and let it out slowly. "I'm ready for another try."

"Very well." Kamara lifted his hands from the controls. "You've got the ship."

"I've got it." *This is going to be really smart, or the dumbest thing I've done since I woke up here.* Bowden reached forward and turned off the nav system.

"*What are you doing?*" Kamara exclaimed. "It will take ten minutes to realign the gyros!"

"I'm going to show you how we do things at the boat," Bowden said absently as he stared at the tumbling asteroid in front of him.

"The boat? I thought you said aircraft *crashed* on the boat!"

"They do, sometimes," Bowden acknowledged. He turned and looked at Kamara, whose eyes were huge. Bowden smiled. "But this isn't one of those times."

Kamara's jaw dropped, but he didn't say anything.

"Hold that thought, and keep your mouth shut," Bowden said with a wink. "I'll show you how we do things the Navy way."

A thought that perhaps his mouth was writing checks his body couldn't cash went through his mind, but he pushed it away as he refocused on the asteroid. *There!* The asteroid reached the right part of its revolution, and he boosted forward. Not having to look at the nav system simplified his scan. Revolution, altitude, closure, lineup. Just like landing on the carrier. *Sort of.*

He looked beyond the asteroid and visualized where he needed to be. Not only did he need to meet it at a certain spot, he needed to be going the right speed to minimize the shock of capture and then give it a pulse to minimize the torque of chasing the arc of rotation as he latched on. He started to drift a little to the left and put in a gentle correction. He fought the urge to flee as the end of the asteroid rotated up toward him like Thor's hammer, ready to smite his ship. Having already seen the sight picture once, though, he was sure he was high enough for it to pass underneath him.

Pretty sure, anyway.

He nulled the drift as he reached the "centerline" position of the "runway" in his mind. The fact that the asteroid didn't spin around its long axis cut down on one of the variables. He'd landed a Hornet on the boat in the North Sea in February, with the ship gyrating in all three axes…this was easier. He forced himself to keep breathing.

The end passed underneath him, and he did a gentle dive as he goosed the ship forward slightly to match the rotation. Lower…a touch faster, then he slapped the Capture button as it illuminated. The magnetic locks grabbed hold, and Bowden had that "car crash" feeling again as the ship took on the rotation of the asteroid.

They were down.

Bowden turned to Kamara. "See. Nothing to it."

Sweat ran up Kamara's face due to centripetal force. It should have brought additional blood flow to his head, too, but the man was strangely white. After a couple of seconds, Kamara shook his head, scattering the beads of sweat, and released his safety belt. "Let's go get a drink," he said. "I need it."

Bowden looked at the starscape rotating in front of him, and the enormity of what he'd just done rushed in on him as the adrenaline left his system. *That wasn't the dumbest thing I've done since I got here; that was the dumbest thing I've ever done.* "Yeah," he said after a moment, a small tremor in his voice. "I need one, too."

Bowden cocked his head. "Here's what I don't understand, though. Why didn't you build a port at the axis of rotation—in the middle of the long dimension? That way, you'd only have to match rotation, and not chase an intercept vector with a constant curve built in?"

Kamara grinned. "Who told you we do not have one there? In fact, that is the location of the primary bay."

"What? Then why are we—"

"To make sure you are the best possible pilot, of course."

* * * * *

Chapter Four

"So," Kamara said three days later as they had lunch in Outpost before their flight, "we're not going to do any more landings on Outpost."

"We're not?" Although the statement should have made Bowden happy—he hated Outpost's capture sequence as it was more dangerous than trapping aboard the carrier, where any landing could be your last—he found that he was truly enjoying the challenge of it. Just like coming aboard the carrier, you got better the more you did it, to the point where—even if you were never truly *comfortable* with it—you accepted the fact that you could do it and lost the sense of fear that assailed you the first twenty or thirty times you willingly threw yourself at a moving deck.

"No, we are done," Kamara said. "You can rendezvous with objects in orbit and you can land on Outpost. Are you ready now for something *truly* challenging?"

"There's something more challenging than those things? What is it, landing on a comet or something?"

Kamara's face fell. "How did you know?"

"How did I know what?"

"That we were going to go to a comet today. Did someone tell you?"

Bowden felt his jaw fall open, and he had to consciously close it. "Seriously? I was just kidding around. Why would we want to go land on a comet?"

Kamara shrugged. "Sometimes they have minerals or ice that is needed at an outpost somewhere. Not this Outpost, but on a station out in the asteroids or beyond that."

"You spend time out beyond the asteroids?"

"Yes," Kamara said with a nod. "If you want to find hidden treasures, you have to look off the traveled path. If you go where no one else has gone, the opportunities there haven't already been picked through."

"That makes sense, I guess." Bowden cocked his head. "So we're really going to land on a comet?"

"Yes we are."

"Why is that harder than landing on Outpost?"

"What do you know about comets?"

"That they're big rocky snowballs left over from the formation of the system. They have tails that point away from the star."

"Why do they have those tails?"

"I'm not an astronomer, but, at a guess, it's because the ice starts heating as the comet approaches the star and the frozen stuff starts melting."

"Yes, but what you are missing from your description is the matter of *scale*. On its approach, the asteroid may be fifteen to twenty-five kilometers wide, but as its orbit brings it near the Sun, it heats up, spewing dust and gases, until it fills an area that is larger than most planets—sometimes up to *fifteen times the size of R'Bak*.

"The process of spewing all that material away is called outgassing and may also result in the comet having a tail one hundred million kilometers long, or longer, due to the effects of solar radiation and the solar wind."

"Do we have to fly through the tail?"

Kamara shook his head. "No, we don't have to fly through either of the tails, although we could if we needed to."

"*Two* tails?"

"Yes. Most comets—the ones that aren't dead because they've outgassed everything they have—actually have two tails: a longer ion tail that interacts with the solar wind and a shorter dust tail made up of smoke-sized dust particles caused by outgassing.

"As I said, we don't have to fly through the tails. We will, however, have to fly through the coma, which is the cloud of water, carbon dioxide, and other gases ejected from the nucleus as it nears the star. Once we are through the coma, we will have to land on the nucleus, and that is where things will get really challenging.

"This is because comet formation is not uniform, nor are the stresses they have been exposed to since their formation. Fracture lines accumulate over time, and heat-induced instability can cause them to give way at unpredictable times and in unpredictable directions. Trying to rendezvous with them is one of the most challenging and dangerous tasks in spaceflight. Imagine rendezvousing with Outpost, but having it rotate in all three directions and not having a docking collar to attach to. Meanwhile, at any moment, it might outgas and spew rocks and debris at your ship, potentially damaging it."

Kamara smiled. "That is what landing on an asteroid is like."

"And you do that *on purpose?*" Bowden asked, horrified. "That sounds like an accident just waiting to happen."

"Well, it's not outgassing *all* the time," Kamara said. "The keys to landing on a comet are to get in and out quickly, and to disturb the surface as little as possible. Oh, and to watch out for any outgassing currently active. You especially don't want to use heavy thrusters near the comet, as you increase your chances of creating a plume exponentially." He shrugged. "Besides that, there's very little chance of anything bad happening. Usually."

"You're not filling me with confidence."

"Really, it's not *that* dangerous. I only know three people who've been hit by outgassing, and two of them survived."

"This doesn't sound like something we ought to be doing."

"Well, it *is* a little more dangerous here than out past the asteroid belt," Kamara said, "as the chances of an outgassing event are a lot higher here due to the proximity of the star." He shrugged again. "Also, Jrar is now close enough that it may cause its own outgassing. There could potentially be three tails—or more—or they could all be twisted into each other. We'll minimize the risk by trying to disturb the comet's nucleus as little as possible. Also, your Colonel Murphy told me you need to be as good a space pilot as possible. If you can land on a comet, you can land anywhere; however, the comet is in the best position today for us to launch and intercept it, so we need to get going."

He turned and started walking, then looked over his shoulder. "Are you coming, then?"

"Yeah," Bowden said as his feet started moving of their own accord. *Why do I feel like I'm about to set a new standard for the dumbest thing I've ever done?*

* * *

"Your controls," Kamara said three days later as they approached the comet's coma. It wasn't as big as it could have been—a lot of the volatiles had blown off the nucleus over the millennia—but there were still almost one thousand kilometers of ionized gasses and detritus to navigate through.

Still, it wasn't as bad as he'd been expecting. Having seen comets from Earth—and worse, the way they were portrayed by Hollywood—he'd expected the tail of the comet to be densely packed. It was anything but. From up close, it was unimpressive; low density material flying in generally the same direction. *Kind of like a U.S. Air Force flyby,* he thought with a chuckle.

Although they didn't, they could have flown through the tail. Yes, they would probably have been hit by a number of fast-moving particles, but it wouldn't have been that many, and the ship could have matched velocities with most of them, limiting their damage.

The coma was different.

"You want me to drive through that?" Bowden asked, looking out the canopy at the ball of gas. Although it wasn't *that* dense, it was still far more abundant than the material in the tails had been, blocking any view of the nucleus. "Aren't you going to do it the first time to show me how it's done?"

Kamara shook his head. "No, it is too dangerous to go through the coma more times than we have to, and you need the experience."

"Are you going to give me some sort of safety brief or anything? Do this? Don't do that?"

Kamara smiled. "Of course; I was just going to do that." He pointed to the coma out Bowden's canopy. "Approach the nucleus. If something gets in our way, avoid it. When we get to the nucleus, avoid any plumes being ejected from it. Fly to within five feet from the nucleus, and I will harpoon it and draw us in." He smiled. "As you say, easy peasy."

"How am I going to see something in our way?"

"Use your radar, of course."

"You make it sound like we've used the radar lots, and it's something I'm comfortable with." Bowden looked down his nose at Kamara. "We haven't, and I'm not."

"Well, now is a great time to get used to it," Kamara said with a smile. "This is what I mostly use it for."

"I just hope it fucking works," Bowden muttered as he flipped the radar on. Systems on Navy aircraft had a habit of breaking when they weren't used. The more you flew and used a system, the better it worked. Don't use it for a few flights in a row? It was unlikely to work when you turned it on.

But—wonder of wonders—the radar began powering up. *There's probably something to be said for not slamming the packet into the deck of a ship over and over that helps with system longevity.* Aside from the module Bowden had crashed the craft into early on, he hadn't really hit anything else "hard."

The radar had two screens: one that showed azimuth distance left or right, and another that showed elevation. In theory, he could do really basic radar nav through the coma when the gasses got too dense. Assuming the radar didn't register all the debris as one giant target.

"Ready?" Kamara asked. "The longer we fly alongside the comet, the longer it will take for us to get back to Outpost."

"Yeah. Here we go." Bowden turned the packet toward the nucleus and boosted toward it, allowing the craft to continue tracking along with its forward velocity.

"You're going to have to go faster than that," Kamara said. For the first time since they'd been flying, he tapped one of the gauges to get Bowden's attention on it. "We're only overtaking it at a rate of about one hundred kilometers an hour," he noted. "It's going to take us ten hours to get there at this rate." He yawned theatrically. "I may have to go to the back and get—or is it *take?*—a nap."

"How fast is too fast?" Bowden asked. "I realize we didn't plan for this to be a two week-long excursion—" *and maybe we should have,* "—but I also don't want to get hit by a big rock fragment that damages the craft."

"The radar has a range of about one hundred kilometers in the average coma. If you go five hundred kilometers an hour, you still have twelve minutes to see and avoid particularly large rocks."

"What about smaller ones that won't be seen until we're in close—or ever? I doubt this radar sees anything fist-sized, but that would leave a large hole through the ship."

"There probably aren't many rocks—"

Clang!

Kamara winced as something hit the packet. "Okay, new plan. Continue inbound at one hundred kilometers per hour, and I'll get a nap. I'll spell you in a couple of hours."

* * *

Kamara peered out the canopy thirteen hours later. They'd had to slow several times as the rocks got larger and denser. "Got anything?"

"No," Bowden replied. "It should be just starboard of the nose, though." He was moving forward at ten kilometers an hour relative velocity, with the nucleus of the comet just over ten kilometers away. He glanced out but didn't see the nucleus either. Kamara had said it was the densest coma he'd ever flown through.

Bowden shook his head. He didn't like flying through the mess; it reminded him too closely of flying near Mount St. Helens after it blew. The ash had stripped all the paint from the nose and leading edges of his aircraft, earning him a visit with the squadron's commanding officer and his opportunity to brief the squadron officers at the next All Officers Meeting about the dangers inherent to flying around erupting volcanoes.

He'd long ago lost the ability to see the stars, and his field of view was nothing more than a diffuse light, like what you'd see walking through a deep fog in the middle of the day. Six kilometers, and he still couldn't see the nucleus visually, although it was obvious on the radar, including a large return on it as if there was a concentration of metal.

Five and a half kilometers, and, if anything, the blasting the packet was getting was even worse. The coma wasn't thinning; the material was getting more dense.

"I don't like this," Bowden said. "I'm going down."

He nudged the thrusters and went "down" and "left" with respect to the comet's nucleus. Within a few seconds, the visibility cleared. It still wasn't great—it was like looking through a thick Los Angeles haze—but he could see the nucleus and the two bright jets spewing material from opposite sides of the vaguely dumbbell-shaped body. They'd been approaching into the ejecta coming from one of them. The nucleus was slowly rotating, so they would have been clear of it eventually; they'd just been unlucky to approach from the wrong direction at the wrong time.

"Good call," Kamara said. "I should have thought of that sooner."

"I wish you had." Bowden's brows knit as he realized the nose kept walking off to the left of the nucleus. *Trust your eyes,* Kamara had said. *What do you do when your eyes are wrong?*

You have other issues, he realized suddenly and looked out at the port wing. The packet was never meant to fly in atmosphere so it wasn't a real 'wing;' it was more of a place to attach things and store propellant. Which was currently leaking out the front of the wing through two small holes. He reached up and turned off the pressurization for the left wing tank, and the leaks slowed.

"What did you do that for?" Kamara asked.

"I've got two leaks in the left wing tank," Bowden replied. "Shit," he added as the nose started walking off to the right. "Looks like there may be one on the right, too."

Kamara looked out his window then reached forward and turned off the pressurization to the right wing tank. "Now I really wish I'd thought of that sooner."

"Still want to do this?"

"No. We need to get out of the coma and repair the tanks. I don't know how much propellant we've lost, but we didn't have a lot to spare."

"*—tance, please help,*" a female voice said over the radio. "*Any station—*" a burst of static interrupted the voice, "*stuck on the comet's nucleus. My ship's damaged—*" another burst of static, "*assistance; please help if possible.*"

Bowden tapped the bright object on the radar. "That's a ship right there. Sounds like she's in trouble."

"You know radar mapping now?"

"Yeah, my plane had it where I came from, and that's something I *do* know. My plane's radar was a lot better than this one, but I trained on a radar something like this as a student." He shrugged. "What's the protocol here? Do we leave to fix our craft or try to render assistance?"

"If we leave, we won't have the fuel to return, and I doubt there's anyone who can get here and back. If we don't help her—whoever she is—she's going to die."

"So we help her."

"We do."

"All right," Bowden said. "Maybe we can make repairs to the tanks while we're down." He shook his head as a third plume of ejecta erupted from the nucleus and its rotation rate sped up. "Assuming we can make it down."

"You can do it," Kamara said. "I have faith in you."

"*Me? Are you kidding?* The ship is damaged, and we have a dangerous landing. Don't you want to land it? It's your ship, after all."

"Have you ever used the harpoon system? Ever tried to attach to a comet before?"

"Well, no."

"I have. You get us close, and I'll tie us in. Try to get us close to the other ship."

Bowden pointed out the canopy. "I can see it now. It's pretty close to one of the jets."

"Get us as close as you can."

"Did you hear what I said?"

"Yes. Stay out of the jet. We've already seen what happens when you fly through that shit. But land close to the other ship. Preferably on a patch of rock."

"Can I ask why?"

"The gravity is going to be minimal on a body that small. If you jump hard, you'll likely jump off it. It will take about two minutes for something to fall from here—" he held his hand at his chest, "to the ground. The less we have to walk around there—much less have a jet open underneath us if you park us on ice—the better."

Bowden felt his eyes open wide as everything hit him all at once. This approach was levels of magnitude harder than landing on Outpost, and yet infinitely more important. Three lives were counting on him flying a "rails" pass, the first time, to a body he'd never approached before.

He swallowed, his mouth suddenly dry. *No pressure there.*

"Got it," he said slowly. "I'll get us close. You bring us in."

"I will."

Kamara nodded and made a radio call while Bowden sized up the approach. The closer he got, the more he decided the asteroid looked like a peanut, with a narrow, elongated middle, than it did a dumbbell. The surface was pitted with huge indentations, although it was impossible to tell whether they were impact craters or cavities formed from the sublimation of material.

He slowed slightly as he got the rhythm of the nucleus' spin.

You can do this. It's a slower rotation than Outpost, and you don't have to hit an exact spot, just a close one. You can do this.

I hope.

* * * * *

Chapter Five

*A*nd...*now.*

    Bowden gave the thrusters a gentle tap and started forward slowly as the nucleus rotated into position. With the body's weird shape, it seemed to wobble slightly as it rotated, and it had taken Bowden a couple of minutes to get the right sight picture on how to approach it.

He nodded his head as the other ship came into view. It was another RockHound packet, although it had a couple of different modules strapped on. Probably gas and prospecting gear, Kamara had said. What it didn't have was right side thrusters, which had obviously been ripped off when the jet had erupted from underneath it. The right wing was a tangled mass of pulverized metal, and the starboard side of the craft showed impacts along its length. It also tilted down on that side.

Bowden gave it no more than a glance as he searched for the spot he'd seen on the previous rotation that was clear of ice. He lined up just to the left of the craft, and there it was—a little in trail of the ship. He gave the thrusters another bump to match the spin of the nucleus and then a nudge to the left to make sure he was clear of the other craft. Within a foot or two of where he wanted to be, he didn't risk over-controlling the craft; he just gave it a tap "down" toward the nucleus.

"Now!" he exclaimed in a tense whisper, almost as if afraid his voice would cause the ship to go off target or open up a jet underneath him—anything to spoil what he'd done to get the craft where it needed to be.

"Standby," Kamara said in a harsh whisper back. "One's locked. Two's locked. Firing!"

He pressed the two buttons and the harpoons lanced out into the rock below them as the craft touched town on the nucleus. The lines retracted as the craft rebounded from the gentle impact and then gently snugged them into place.

"Fuck," Bowden said as he let out the breath he'd been unconsciously holding. "That's an approach I hope to never have to repeat."

"You need to fly with us RockHounds more," Kamara said with a half-smile. "We do all the fun flying."

"You can keep it." Bowden's visor had been starting to fog, but now that he was breathing a bit more normally, it cleared quickly. "What now?"

"I talked to the woman on the radio while you ran the approach. Her name is Malanye Raptis. She landed on the nucleus without any problems, but a jet opened up next to her and destroyed her craft. She had just about given up when I called her.

"I don't want to stay here any longer than we have to; it's too unstable. Unfortunately, though, our trip here is going to necessitate some repairs and we're going to need more fuel to get back. On the good side, I have a repair kit and Raptis has plenty of fuel she isn't going to be needing anymore. While I fix our ship, why don't you go to her ship and help her bring the fuel over? She said she would meet you at the boarding ladder."

"Sure thing." Bowden stood up slowly to keep from bouncing off the ceiling. There was indeed gravity on the nucleus, but, as

Kamara had warned, it was extremely light. What Kamara hadn't mentioned was that "down" wasn't actually straight down. Due to the comet's shape, gravity actually pulled him down and to the side slightly. The pull wasn't strong, but it was enough to be a little disconcerting and disorienting.

Having gotten used to operating in zero-g conditions over the last several weeks, though, having a little gravity made things marginally easier as there *was* a little "down" to help with momentum control. You didn't lose your mass with weightlessness, so stopping in zero-g was difficult. On the ground, you used friction to stop, but if you tried to stop against the floor in space you just bounced off it—there was nothing to hold you to it. He quickly found that the only way you stopped was by grabbing onto something, and he understood why the astronauts always seemed to move slowly on the space shuttle. Pushing off hard meant you had a significantly greater impact with whatever you were aiming at, and you ran the risk of breaking bones and dislocating joints when you tried to stop yourself.

Operating in heavy suits only increased your mass and made the resulting impact even more brutal. You had to move carefully or you ran the risk of killing yourself.

Bowden exited through the airlock and climbed carefully down the ladder to the surface. Heeding Kamara's warning, he moved cautiously across the intervening fifty meters to the other ship. His eyes wanted to focus on the erupting matter pouring from the comet and follow it up and away from the surface, until it was lost in the fog above them, and he had to focus his vision on the craft to keep from getting overwhelmed by the display.

The initial eruption had started next to her craft, but it had wandered down the seam and was now about twenty meters on the far side of the packet. He kept telling himself that, while the jet was close enough to be a distraction—and a real danger if the jet should move back closer again—it was not something he had to worry about. Be aware of, yes, but not worry about. Somehow simply knowing the distinction existed didn't make it believable in his mind.

He made it to the ship and climbed the ladder to find a space-suited woman waiting for him. She was dark-haired and considerably shorter than Bowden. After a couple of seconds staring at her, not knowing what to do, she tapped the side of her head and held up three fingers. Bowden turned his suit radio to channel three. "Hi," he said, unsure of how to continue. When she looked at him strangely, he smiled and added in the local SpinDog lingo, "I'm Kevin Bowden."

"Thank you for coming," the woman replied in SpinDog. "I'm Malanye Raptis." She cocked her head at him. "Wait. You are one of the…Terrans? What are you doing out here?" She craned her head to the side to look around him. "And what are you doing with a Rock-Hound ship?"

"I was training with Kamara when we heard your distress call, and we came to help. He's fixing our ship—we took some damage on the way in here—and he sent me to see if you had fuel you could spare."

The woman laughed. "I do, and it isn't doing me much good here. We can run hoses over to your ship. I will attach them. Meet me underneath the port wing."

"Okay," Bowden said, and he went back down the ladder and stood under the wing. Most of the area was ice, and he moved to the single rocky spot visible. Then he realized the rock might be like the cork in a pressurized bottle, just waiting to blow off, and he stepped back to the ice…which he realized was even more likely to blow off. He stepped back onto the rock and sighed, saying a quick prayer that the whole area would remain stable for a few minutes longer.

Waiting gave him a moment to study his surroundings, and he shook his head as the enormity was almost enough to overwhelm him. He was the first human to stand on a comet. Well, the first he knew of, anyway. No telling what the people on Earth had done in the couple of centuries since he'd been abducted.

Without warning, a ten-centimeter-diameter hose drifted down from above. He started to reach out and catch it, but then caught himself. Having no idea what it was made of—and therefore its mass—he let it drift to the ground. It made a big cloud of ice crystals when it hit; it had massed more than he'd originally thought.

After another minute, a second hose came down, followed by Raptis. Her suit gave a small braking jet just before she touched down, then she dropped the last few centimeters gracefully.

"Well, what are you waiting for?" she asked. "Grab a hose. We need to get the fuel out of my ship before the jet decides to come back over here and finish what it started." She picked up one of the hose ends and began trudging toward Kamara's ship.

Bowden grabbed the other one after a couple of seconds and followed in her footsteps, trying to mimic her flowing, slightly bouncing steps that allowed her to go a lot faster than Bowden's earlier cautious pace.

Kamara was on the starboard wing when they arrived. He tapped the side of his head and held his arms out to the side, palms up. Raptis held up three fingers, and Kamara joined them on the frequency. "Just finishing up here. What took you so long?"

"Your student is about as useful—and as space-acclimated—as a newborn," Raptis replied.

"You might want to speak a little nicer about him," Kamara replied. "He's the one who said we needed to come get you, and the one who piloted my ship to get us here."

"He did?" A new note of appreciation tempered her tone.

"Yes."

The woman sighed over the connection. "Well, it *was* a nice landing," she admitted.

"Ready," Kamara said. He stood at the wing's edge, holding out his hands.

Raptis coiled up some extra hose and then tossed up the end she was holding. Five meters above her, Kamara braced himself and caught the end. The hose snaked upward as he went to attach it to the fuselage. He returned a minute later and held out his hands again. "Ready for the other."

Knowing it was coming, Bowden had coiled it like Raptis had done, but his toss wasn't as accurate, and the slightly different gravity pulled it away from the craft. Kamara leaned out but wasn't able to reach it.

"Want me to do it?" Raptis asked.

"No," Bowden replied, unwilling to admit he wasn't up to the task. He coiled it again, looked up to see that Kamara was in position, and tossed it up again. This time, he adjusted for the altered gravity by aiming at the tip of the wing. It drifted away—missing it by a centimeter or two—and rose to where Kamara could grab it. He went to attach it to the craft.

Bowden turned to Raptis, satisfaction in his eyes, only to receive a vision of her backside as she walk-bounced back toward her ship.

Bowden shook his head then chuckled. *Leave it to an aviator to turn hose tossing into a macho competition.*

"What else do you need me to do?" Bowden asked.

"Get back to the cockpit and be ready to flip the switches when I tell you to."

"You got it." Bowden went back through the airlock and sat in the pilot's seat. He'd never done a refueling before—normally, the station's ground crew handled it—but he was able to follow along and flip the switches for Kamara when he called for them. Fifteen minutes later, they were almost finished. Raptis had brought extra fuel with her, expecting to return from much further away, and it was enough to completely fill Kamara's ship. During that time, Raptis had made two trips between the ships.

"Emergency breakaway!" Kamara yelled. "Emergency breakaway. Turn off all switches!"

Bowden's hand flew across the panel. "They're off!" he called back.

"Disconnecting!" he shouted.

Bowden hurried to the starboard window and looked back. His eyes widened, and his mouth dropped open in horror. The ejecta jet had returned to Raptis' craft and blown it upward off the comet. Kamara had disconnected one hose, and it snaked back toward the ship while Kamara wrestled with the other, held taut as Raptis' ship pulled away from them.

Kamara's ship shifted, and it creaked as the wires held it in place. Bowden stared, unable to figure out anything he could do to help. Which would break first? The wires holding Kamara's ship? The hose? Something in Kamara's ship? Bowden had no idea.

Finally, Kamara succeeded in detaching the hose, but it snapped up, smashed into his faceplate, and hurled him up off the wing. Motion from the ground caught his eye as Raptis launched herself up after the cartwheeling Kamara.

"Kamara, come in!" Bowden called. No response. "Kamara, are you okay?" Still no response.

"I'm tracking him," Raptis said, "but I don't have much fuel in my suit. I can get him, but you're going to have to come get us. I don't have enough to return."

"Shit," Bowden said. "Shit, shit, shit." *Kamara gone; maybe dead. Raptis gone Dutchman in space after him. What do I do?*

"First things first," he muttered. "Gotta go after them. Start ship."

He ran through the ship's start-up sequence, once again wishing for a checklist to ensure he didn't forget anything. He got two steps reversed and had to go back and redo them. *If I get out of this, I am by God putting together a checklist.*

Bowden finally got the motors going but the ship wouldn't lift off. *Damn it, the harpoons!* He shuffled over to the other seat and looked at the harpoon panel. The button with the cover caught his eye. Emergency Release. *Perfect.* He flipped up the cage over it and mashed the button. He felt two *pops!* then the ship started drifting away from the comet…heading toward the eruption that had already claimed Raptis' ship. He pushed off toward the other side of the cockpit, harder than he'd intended, and crashed into the port window, bruising his left forearm. As he rebounded, he snagged his seat and pulled himself into it.

He tried to attach his straps, but his left arm burned like fire every time he moved it. He settled for only latching the lap belt, which would at least hold him in place, and concentrated on flying.

* * * * *

Chapter Six

Bowden realized he'd damaged his left arm more than he thought as he steered the packet up and away from the jet blowing debris from the comet. Every movement hurt, but he couldn't think about it—he had to find Kamara and Raptis.

Which was probably going to be impossible since the stupid RockHounds were too worried about staying unseen to have handy little things like a Blue Force Tracker or some other locator he could have used to zero in on them.

He visually searched the coma, looking for them in the haze, but they were nowhere in sight. Belatedly, he realized they'd been ejected off in a different trajectory than he'd lifted off in, and he spun the craft around to an approximate heading of where he'd thought they'd gone.

Still nothing.

I could wander around in the coma forever and never find them, he realized. *Would they still remain caught in the comet's gravity, or did they have enough escape velocity to break free?* He had no idea. *What did he have that could find them?*

The radar. He'd found the nucleus with it; maybe he could find the two suits with it. Sure, the radar was shit, but he could differentiate the metal of their thruster packs from the generic bits of rock flying around, and they weren't in the debris being spewed out, so they ought to stand out a little more clearly. He flipped the radar on and waited impatiently as it warmed up.

After a subjective eternity waiting, the picture finally formed on the screen. Nothing. Some small, fuzzy returns that were probably rocks, but nothing that looked like refined metal.

Think, Bowden, think. Why don't you see them?

They're not there, obviously.

Why not?

They're somewhere else, obviously.

But where?

He opened up the scope to scan the most volume possible. Still nothing.

You need to set up a scan pattern, just as if you were looking for enemy fighters.

As soon as he had the thought, he realized the problem—he wasn't looking in three dimensions. He was certain—well, *mostly* certain—he was on the right general azimuth; he might just not be looking high or low enough. Space was big—too big for one small radar to look everywhere. He needed a better scan pattern. He hadn't flown very far above the comet, so he gently pitched the nose of the craft up and panned it from side to side.

Still nothing.

A little more pitch, and re-scan.

This time he got two blips.

Gotcha.

He tapped the thrusters, wanting to get there immediately, but also knowing he'd have to match velocities with them when he found them. As he approached, one of the blips resolved into two blips, very close together. *That's them!*

As he got closer, the coma thinned a little, and he could see them. One was holding onto the other. As carefully as he could, he slid into position next to them. One of the figures waved, then pointed at the packet, then pointed back at the two figures.

That must be Raptis, and she wants me to come get them.

Oh, hell.

Bowden snuggled the craft up to the two figures and saw one of them holding up three fingers.

He looked at his suit; somehow the controls had switched to channel four. He switched it back to three. "Hi y'all. Need a ride?"

"Yes," Raptis said. "Kamara is unconscious, and I'm out of thruster fuel. Get out here and get us."

"On my way." He unstrapped and went to the airlock, trying to ignore the pain in his arm. As he cycled it open, he searched for the suited figures, but didn't immediately see them. Panic started to set in, but then he caught motion from the corner of his eye. *They were holding onto the wing!*

Whether it was the coma blocking the blackness of space or his haste to get out to them, he forgot to feel overwhelmed—like he usually did—and released his hold on the airlock and jetted away from the ship.

Every motion he made set his left arm on fire, reminding him to keep his approach slow and under control. Raptis pushed off gently from the wing so he'd have a bigger target to aim for, and he intercepted the pair. Pushing the group of them with his thrusters took a good bit of experimentation and flailing around—which wasn't helped by Raptis' biting comments on thruster control—but eventually, he got them back to the airlock and inside.

"Glad you found us," Raptis said once they had Kamara inside the packet and strapped down. She took off his helmet and held it up to show it had several pieces of tape across it. "He wouldn't have lasted much longer. I did my best to seal the holes in his helmet and suit, but he was still losing air."

"Sorry it took me so long to find you," Bowden replied. "You had spun off into the coma before I could get the ship fired up, and I had to use the radar to find you."

"You used the radar?" she asked. "And you were able to find us…"

"Yeah." Bowden gave her a wry smile. "Sorry if there was a better way; it was all I could think of."

Raptis shook her head. "No. That was a great way to do it; I'm not sure I would have thought to do it that way." She cocked her head. "That's the second time you've saved my life today. You know, you're not too bad…for a Terran."

"Well, thanks." He chuckled. "I think."

"Why don't you go fly us home now?" she asked. Raptis was all business again; the moment was over. "I will do what I can for Kamara."

"Uh, yeah, sure." Bowden stood in the hatchway a moment, not sure he should leave Kamara in case there was something he needed to do for him.

Raptis looked up after a moment. "He will need competent medical treatment. The sooner you get us back to Outpost, the sooner he'll get it."

"Oh, yeah." Bowden turned toward the cockpit. He was halfway there before he realized he had no idea how he was going to find Outpost again without Kamara.

* * * * *

Chapter Seven

"Welcome back," Murphy said a week later as he sat down at the table aboard *Spin One* where Bowden was eating lunch. "How'd it go?"

"Good, sir," the aviator replied, "even if it wasn't without some challenges." He explained the trip to the comet and how he had—eventually and with some coaching—returned to Outpost. They'd spent a couple days there while they got treatment for their injuries, then he'd flown them back to *Spin One*.

"Speaking of challenges," Murphy said with a smile, "I heard you had fun with your first rendezvous with an orbiting object."

"That was one of them." Bowden chuckled ruefully. "How did you hear about that? Kamara said he wasn't going to mention that to you."

"Nothing travels through the hab like a good rumor." Murphy winked. "The fact that you destroyed his rangefinder was quite the topic of conversation for a few days." Murphy chuckled like Bowden had. "He didn't tell me, by the way. I had a bet with one of the SpinDogs that you'd ace it on your first approach. That's how the rumors got started. He'd never won a bet from me before."

"Oops, sorry, sir." Bowden winced. "I hope it didn't cost you much."

"Nope." Murphy smiled. "I bet him twice as much that you'd be able to land on Outpost within your first two tries."

Bowden shook his head. "You had a lot of confidence in me. I'm not sure I'd have made that bet." He smiled. "I'm also glad I wasn't aware of the bet until afterward. I had enough pressure on me at the time."

"I knew you'd come through." He nodded. "By the way, Kamara said you're 'the best student he's ever had.'"

Bowden's eyes opened wide. "Really? He said that?"

"Yeah. Apparently, he was pretty impressed with your skills. Finding his floating body with your radar, then rendezvousing with it and saving him may have had something to do with it."

"Huh." Bowden shrugged. "Raptis saved him—she dove off the comet after him and sealed his suit, or he never would have made it." He shook his head. "Based on how he treated me, I never would have guessed I was better than a RockHound five year old. That's what he said, anyway."

"It's true." Murphy's face got serious, and he rubbed his left hand absently. "You ready for more? Launches to space and re-entries?"

"Absolutely. I can't be a full-up astronaut unless I can do launches and re-entries."

Murphy indicated the mostly empty refectory with a sweep of his right hand. "Some people would say you're already an astronaut. You *are* in space, after all."

Bowden shrugged. "I'll consider myself an astronaut after I've been at the controls for a round trip. Every other time I've been down to the planet and back, I've just been baggage, and while I've been here, I was more of a tourist. Astronauts *do* things in space."

Murphy smiled. "Like land ships on tumbling asteroids like Outpost?"

"Exactly. You don't have to tell Kamara how scared I was the first time I did it."

"I won't." He winked. "Based on what he told me, he was a lot more scared than you were."

Bowden shrugged. "I was in the zone. Sometimes, when you're behind the ship, everything just works as if you're on rails. Airspeed, angle of attack, lineup…they're all 'on,' and it's as if you didn't have to put any conscious thought into keeping them there. There was never a doubt in my mind."

"Is that pilot bravado or do you think you can do it again without anyone there to hold your hand?"

"It's not just pilot bravado." Bowden chuckled. "Well, not much, anyway. I did another ten landings on Outpost after that pass. Only took me thirteen attempts to get ten landings, which Kamara did say was better than most of the RockHounds can do. I nailed the one coming back from the comet, too, even with a hairline fracture in my left arm."

"Ten out of thirteen makes you better than most?" Murphy asked. "It must be hard."

"It is, but then again, so is landing on an aircraft carrier in heavy seas, and Navy pilots have gotten…well, when we got snatched, we were pretty good at it. No telling what they're doing now back home."

"Maybe we'll find out," Murphy said. "But before we can…"

"You have a new mission for me?"

"I will. For now, though, you still have more training to do."

"Still can't tell me what the mission is?"

"No, I can't share it yet as the walls here have ears, but things are in motion, and I need you trained ASAP. Maybe sooner than that. I need you to concentrate on becoming the best astronaut pilot you can be, as quickly as you can do it."

"Well, I've had worse jobs," Bowden said. He smiled. "This is better than flying for the Navy."

"How so?"

"Back on the ship, when you got back from flying, you had a ground job you had to put hours into. Here? All I have to do is fly and get better at it. I love my job."

"Well, good. Just keep—" He broke off and waved to someone behind Bowden. "Here's someone you know."

Bowden turned to find Burg Hrensku walking toward him. "Hi, Burg. What are you doing here?"

"Hello," the SpinDog said. "Apparently, I am to be your next instructor. Primus Anseker asked me to help out." He shrugged. "When the Primus asks..."

"You say yes."

"Well, I'll leave you two to get on with it," Murphy said, standing. He glanced down at Bowden and held the gaze for an extra couple of seconds, giving it significance. "Quickly." He nodded once, a quick jerk of his head. "I've got other stuff to get back to." He left and Hrensku sat down in Murphy's spot.

"So," Hrensku said, "I know you've been on a number of runs to the planet and back. What is most important about performing a re-entry?"

Bowden chuckled. "I was riding in the back for all but the last trip up, so I wouldn't say I've got a lot of experience doing it." He pondered the question a moment. "Slowing down and landing in one piece?"

Hrensku smiled. "You're not wrong, but that was not what I was asking. How do we get from space safely through the atmosphere so that we *can* land in one piece?"

"I'm sorry, but I never went through astronaut training. I can modify and fly aircraft, and now I know how to fly spacecraft *in space*, but I don't know how to transition a spacecraft into an aircraft." He gave Hrensku a wry grin. "I was kind of hoping you'd teach me that."

"I will, but I wanted to see what you knew, first."

"Well, based on the spacecraft piloting I've done, I know you need to slow down to go lower, so I imagine it starts with going slower."

"Correct. Besides, if you go too fast, you'll bounce off the atmosphere and go flying off into space, never to return."

"I will?" Bowden asked, horrified at the thought.

Hrensku laughed. "No, you won't go flying off into space. We always tell the new trainees that, though, to see their reactions."

Bowden chuckled self-deprecatingly. "Okay, you got me. So you can't skip off the atmosphere."

"Oh, no, you totally *can* skip off the atmosphere," Hrensku said.

"But wait—"

"—you just don't keep going into space," Hrensku finished. "If you don't slow down enough for atmospheric penetration, you can bounce off, but you are still in orbit. You will go back up partway toward where you started, and it may take you a while to get back down to the atmosphere again, but you don't fly off into space. You just end up at a lower orbit than where you started.

"If you are performing a re-entry, the two most important things to doing it successfully are your velocity and the entry angle with respect to the local horizon. These two things need to be within the limits of your craft or bad things happen.

"We'll talk about velocity first. As you already mentioned, it's a major factor. If you are going too fast, the thermal loads and braking forces will overwhelm your heat shield. Once the heat shield fails…"

"You burn up," Bowden said with a nod. "How fast are you talking?"

"Typically, from a low orbit, the velocity is around eight kilometers per second, but you also need to have the correct entry angle. If the entry angle is too steep, the braking effect due to atmospheric friction will become too large and the spacecraft can break up. Additionally, the steeper the entry angle, the higher the heat. Once again, if the heat exceeds what the shield can take, you will either get burn-throughs or the heat shield will fail entirely."

Bowden nodded. "And your crispy remains will fall to Earth. I mean the planet's surface."

"Correct."

"And, let me guess, based on your earlier comment, that it can't be too shallow, either, or other bad things happen."

"You are correct again," Hrensku said. "At a shallower angle, the deceleration won't be enough, and the spacecraft will travel much farther than it is supposed to. You might not be able to make it back to where you intended to land…or even find a spot where you are able to land. Additionally, even though the heat shield will be exposed to a lower amount of heat, it will be exposed for a much longer time, which may result in a larger total heat load. No matter how good the shield, at some point, you're going to burn away all the protective insulation. Whether that results in burn-throughs or heat seeping through the shield, making the temperatures inside the spacecraft too high, neither is pleasant."

"And both are probably fatal," Bowden opined.

"Correct. Also, if the entry angle is really shallow, you again run the risk of bouncing off the atmosphere and continuing with your orbit. This results in an elliptical orbit, and when you come back down, you'll be in a different place than you'd planned, probably nowhere near your intended reentry corridor."

Bowden nodded. "So we end up landing somewhere far, far away."

"Probably." He shrugged. "For reentry, accurate guidance and control is extremely important."

Bowden took a deep breath and let it out slowly. "I see." He shrugged. "So how do we figure all that out?"

Hrensku stood. "Come with me, and I will show you."

* * *

I can't believe this is how we do it, Bowden said to himself for at least the tenth time as they prepared to de-orbit. Hrensku had shown him that they had a computer in the craft that *could* calculate the navigational data for the return trip. For some reason, though—and Hrensku didn't want to talk about it any more than Kamara had—they weren't big on autonomous programs and didn't use them unless some sort of emergency required them to do so.

Not that it was much of a computer in any event. If Bowden had to compare it to something from his time, it was most like the computer in the A-6E Intruders from his airwing. Their computers operated at four hertz. The Intruder guys had joked, somewhat sarcastically, that it updated four times a second, "whether it needed to or not." The programming in the interface craft's computers might have helped NASA in the Sixties and early Seventies, but operating it would have been a lot like the first round of computer games he had played—uncomplicated and not entirely satisfying.

But that would have been better than the actual method the SpinDogs used. He'd been fairly horrified when he'd found out what was going to determine whether he lived or died on reentry. Hrensku was going to "eyeball it in."

Too bad we can't use the technology the Dornaani left us to do it better and smarter. He'd asked Murphy about it and was told the cultural backlash for using the technology they had access to would probably have led to several hundred of the SpinDogs dead and all the Lost Soldiers on a forever stroll beyond the airlocks—without benefit of vacc suits.

"The 1960s called," Bowden muttered. "They want their computers back. Sad thing is, I do, too."

"What was that?" Hrensku asked.

"Nothing," Bowden said louder. "I'm ready for the checklist."

"Checklist?"

"Yeah. Don't you have a checklist to make sure you don't forget anything?"

"Of course there's one, but I have it memorized. I know what I'm supposed to do."

"How do you know you won't forget a step?"

Hrensku tapped his forehead. "It is all here. Papers can be forgotten."

"It would be easier on a slate."

"And what if you had your list on a computer and it suddenly malfunctioned or ran out of power? You wouldn't know what to do. *I will.*"

"But what if—?" Bowden stopped himself. Approaching reentry was the wrong time to argue the merits of having written checklists. Certainly, Hrensku had already shown he wasn't interested in having the checklist on a tablet computer—an electronic flight bag—and he wouldn't permit Bowden to even have one in *his* interface craft. "Never mind," Bowden said. "So what do we do?"

"First we close all the doors and hatches." Hrensku flipped a couple of switches and pointed to a section of the control panel where six lights glowed dimly. One was red, but after a couple of seconds, it went green. "All set."

Hrensku pointed. "Flip the switch over there that says 'toilet.'"

"Toilet?"

"Yes. It shuts the toilet and seals all the contents."

"Got it," Bowden said. *Also added to the checklist I'm going to make.*

Hrensku flipped the switch that brought up the craft's gyro display. Typically, the SpinDog pilot had no use for it—and said repeatedly that it was better to not use it as a crutch—but it was marginally acceptable to use it for getting the right attitude for reentry. A small picture of the interface craft and a tunnel-like image filled the center screen. The display looked like something out of *Star Wars*, but designed by a five year old who had little concept of what he was trying to depict.

Hrensku pointed to the left screen—the one with the image of the craft—which now showed two of the craft on it. "The red image shows the craft's current attitude," Hrensku noted, "while the green one shows the attitude the craft needs to be in for reentry. I must maneuver the craft to superimpose the 'actual' craft onto the one representing the optimal attitude for reentry."

Would it have been child's play to design a computer program to accomplish the maneuver?

Yes.

Was doing so somehow anathema to the SpinDogs?

Also yes.

Bowden sighed to himself as Hrensku manipulated the controls and brought the craft into alignment with the desired attitude at almost the same time an image of the craft appeared at the end of the tunnel on the right half of the screen. The craft was shown above the tunnel.

"See?" Hrensku asked. "As expected, we are above our projected velocity. We must slow down." He fired the craft's main thrusters. After a couple of seconds, the image on the display began to drop into the tunnel. When it got to the center of the tunnel, Hrensku shut down the thrusters. Immediately, the green image on the left flipped around.

"Braking is complete," Hrensku advised. "Now we adopt our reentry attitude."

"How long do you have to do it?"

"It is not a race. We have about twenty minutes until we reach the edge of the atmosphere." He shrugged. "You should do it this time." He removed his hands from the controls. "Your craft."

A little warning would have been nice. "My craft," Bowden said, taking the stick. He then manipulated the thrusters until the two images on the left screen superimposed. The bottom of the craft was now aligned nose-first with respect to their orbit, with the nose pitched upward. The view out the side of the craft showed they were on the opposite side of the planet from where they were headed.

"Oh, I forgot," Hrensku said. "You need to burn off the gas in the forward reaction control system."

"Oh?"

"Yes. It is a safety precaution because that area experiences the highest heat of re-entry."

"A checklist could be used to remember this," Bowden muttered.

"What was that?"

"I said, 'won't firing the thrusters mess up our flight path and our attitude?'"

"Yes, it will. You will need to counter it with the aft thrusters."

"Wonderful," Bowden muttered. "Dumbest system ever."

"What was that?"

"Nothing. I'm concentrating. What powers the thrusters?"

"Nitrogen tetroxide is the oxidizer, and monomethyl hydrazine is the fuel. The propellants are hypergolic—they ignite when they come into contact with each other."

"I know what hypergolic is."

"Oh, good. Well, they are fed into the engines, where they atomize, ignite, and produce gas and thrust."

"And we'd be a lot better off without a bunch of them some-where that is about to get really hot."

"Correct."

"That's a stupid system," Bowden muttered.

"What was that?"

"I can see why we'd want to get rid of them," Bowden replied as he worked the controls to burn off the propellants, while still keeping the craft's attitude relatively stable. Dust started falling slowly past his face. "Is that gravity returning?"

"Yes, we are starting to feel it more. I've got the controls."

"You've got the controls," Bowden replied.

A glow to his left caused Bowden to look out the window again. The sky had become a light pink, and, as he watched, it became a deeper pinkish red. He glanced at the display; Hrensku had the craft centered in the display. The glow from the window brightened visibly, going from red to orange.

"Looks like we're in the atmosphere," Bowden noted. He hadn't felt nervous before, but now there was a whole swarm of butterflies in his stomach. Or was that gravity returning with more force? It felt more like butterflies.

"Yes," Hrensku said, his voice a little louder. "Compression and friction are heating the air around us. Right now you're in the middle of a three-thousand-degree fireball."

Yep. Definitely butterflies.

"Even if we wanted to, we couldn't call anyone; the radios will be out for another ten minutes due to the ionization effects."

Unlike the movies he'd seen, there was very little feeling—no shaking or vibration—just the glow of the massive amounts of heat being generated by the interface craft's atmospheric entry. He should have known Hollywood would make it worse than it was. He'd pictured the shuttle almost falling apart; the reality was much less scary…until he thought about the massive amounts of heat being held at bay only a few meters away, and the butterflies returned.

Eventually, the glow faded, and Hrensku waggled the wings. "I have atmospheric control," he reported as he initiated the series of S-turns shown on the screen.

"Are we going to light the engines?" Bowden asked.

"You don't want to fly a glider?" Hrensku asked with a smile.

"Not if I don't have do."

Hrensku sighed theatrically. "If you insist." He flipped the switches and relit the motors, although he kept them at idle. "Still have a lot of velocity to bleed off." He pointed out the window. "There's the field. Want to land it?"

"Me?"

"Sure. You can land it, right?"

"Well, yeah, sure. I've done it lots of times. Just never after a flight to space."

"Unless you land like a glider—which we're not—it's the same thing."

"I've got the controls," Bowden said.

"You have the controls."

Bowden continued to do S-turns to slow the craft and then brought the throttles up slowly to bring the craft into the powered flight regime. Although he felt like it should have been different, the craft flew just like it had the last time he'd flown it in atmosphere. He brought it in to land, taxied to the makeshift base operations building, then powered it down and started the fifteen-minute wait while the craft cooled and the gases created on reentry dissipated.

Bowden released his seatbelt and tried to stand, but only made it about halfway up before falling back into the seat.

"That is one of the hardest things about returning to the planet," Hrensku said. "Readapting from zero gravity is difficult, especially if you've been gone a while."

"Which I have."

"Just go slowly, and it will come back to you."

* * * * *

Chapter Eight

"Ready to go?" Hrensku asked several days later as they walked out to the interface craft for Bowden's first launch to space at the controls.

"Yeah," Bowden said with a chuckle. "I finally just got readjusted to gravity again; must be time to leave."

"Just so. Such is the life of an interface pilot." He glanced at Bowden out of the corner of his eye. "Is that what they have planned for you? To be the Lost Soldiers' interface pilot?"

Bowden shrugged. "I don't know what they have in store for me."

"There must be something you Terrans are planning. To need these qualifications all of a sudden speaks to there being something going on."

"Maybe." Bowden shrugged. "If there is, though, I don't know what it is."

They put their gear in the craft and did the aircraft's preflight while the loadmasters finished stowing the cargo. Although there wasn't going to be anyone else on the craft with them, they were going back fully loaded with medicinals, food, and other stores for the habitats.

The preflight was fairly normal—a small leak to be fixed and a couple of bolts to be tightened—until they got to the cockpit. The landing gear lever was missing the round ball-like attachment on the end that was used to grip it, leaving just a metal post sticking out of the instrument panel.

Bowden got down on his hands and knees and searched the cockpit but couldn't find it.

"It's not necessary," Hrensku said after five minutes of searching. "We'll get a replacement at the spin when we get there."

"That isn't what we'd do back home," Bowden replied. "If something was missing from the cockpit, the aircraft would be down until they found the missing item."

He looked up to find Hrensku looking at him funny. "Down?" Hrensku asked. "Where would it go down to?"

Bowden chuckled. "Not physically down. The word in that case means 'not flyable' until they found the missing piece. We didn't want it to get into the controls and bind something."

"In this case, it is all right," Hrensku replied. "The piece is big enough that it couldn't have gotten into anything."

"Where did it go then?"

"Who knows? Maybe someone took it as a souvenir."

"A souvenir? Why would someone take that?"

"Who is to say?" Hrensku shrugged. "This is the only craft, though, so we either take it or we don't go flying today. And, if we don't hurry, we're going to miss our launch window."

"Okay," Bowden said slowly, not feeling entirely comfortable with it. Navy procedures were typically written in blood. If there was a procedure that *had* to be followed, that usually meant the reason for implementing the procedure was because someone had died. He shook off his misgivings—there really was no place for the knob to go in the cockpit; perhaps it had gotten loose and someone had taken it before it fell off.

They strapped in, fired up the craft, and taxied to the runway. They stopped just short of it so the maintenance crew could arm the RATO—the rocket-assisted takeoff—bottles. As conventional take-off consumed a great deal of their dual-phase engines' fuel—limiting cargo capacity to twenty percent of what can be lifted with RA-TOs—the interface craft usually used the rockets to get airborne and on their way to space.

"Your controls," Hrensku said as the maintenance guys moved away from the craft. The leader held up two pins to show both bottles had been armed.

"My controls," Bowden replied. Sweat prickled across his skin. Although he'd done RATO takeoffs before, usually the SpinDogs supplied the pilot for any RATO takeoffs. While they were fairly common, they were also dangerous, and there were a lot of opportunities for things to go wrong.

Bowden took a deep breath and visualized what he needed to do. In some respects, the RATO takeoff was similar to launching from a carrier. Once the button was pushed, there was no stopping until the assist was over. With a RATO, though, you actually rotated the air-craft while still boosting, so you had to make sure your seat was close enough to the instrument panel to reach everything. It was somewhat worrisome that the landing gear lever in front of him didn't have the ball on the end of it, but once the gear was up, it wouldn't be pointed at him anymore.

"Well?" Burg asked. "We're going to miss our launch window."

"Keep your pants on," Bowden muttered.

"Why would I remove them?" Burg asked.

"It's just an expression…never mind."

He checked the runway and taxied out onto it. Bowden shrugged his shoulders, making sure the straps were set. "Ready?"

"I have been," Hrensku grumbled. "Can we go now?"

"Sure." Bowden put his finger over the RATO button. "Three, two, one." He mashed the button and was pushed back into his seat. The force, however, wasn't what it should have been. As the craft roared down the runway, it pushed against his control, trying to go to the right. The right rocket bottle had failed.

"Bad rocket!" Hrensku called.

"No shit," Bowden muttered. He pulled back the throttles and fought to keep the aircraft on the runway. "Keep your damn hands off," Bowden yelled as Hrensku's hands moved toward the controls. "My plane."

The craft streaked down the runway, and he had to keep forward pressure on the stick and pop the spoilers as their speed increased past the point where the craft was going fast enough to fly, and it tried to get airborne. As they passed the halfway marker—six thousand feet remaining—the operational bottle went out. It would be close, but Bowden knew he could still stop the aircraft.

He pressed the brakes while keeping the spoilers up. Nothing happened. He released the brakes then jumped on them as hard as he could. The right one grabbed for a second, then it blew. The strut slammed into the ground and then ripped off, dropping the wing into contact with the ground.

Bowden was thrown out of his seat and into the port window. There was an instant of pain, then everything went black.

* * * * *

Chapter Nine

Bowden opened his eyes to see Captain Dave Fiezel, a former F-105F pilot in another time and place, walking into his room. Bowden's eyes widened; this wasn't his room—*where was he?*

Everything snapped back. The takeoff. Rockets failing and brakes squealing. Going off the runway. Pain. Lots of pain. Blackness.

"Where—where am I?"

"You're in the infirmary," Fiezel said. "Don't you remember?"

"The crash? Yeah, I remember the crash. I hurt all over."

"You're lucky to still be here to feel pain."

"Why's that?"

Fiezel looked around and his brows knit. "Hasn't anyone told you?"

"Just woke up…I think. Told me what?"

"Uh…"

"Out with it," Bowden said. He was obviously on pain meds of some sort, because his thoughts were mushy and thinking was hard. The act of concentrating, though, brought things more into focus. "Told me what?"

"The only reason you're alive is that the tire blew. The landing gear knob was missing. If you hadn't been thrown to the side—up against the window—the sudden stop when you went off the runway would have impaled you on the lever. It would have gone right through your chest. As it was, it went into the meat of your arm. It still nicked your brachial artery, though, which almost killed you. They had to bring in one of the local witch doctors to use some of their magic weeds on you. Your recovery is nothing short of miraculous, according to our medic types."

Bowden looked down; his right arm was a mass of bandages.

"You'll be fine. It'll hurt a while, and you'll have to work it back into shape, but you're going to be all right." He took a breath as if he were going to add something else but then sighed.

"What?" Bowden asked.

"Not sure it's my place to say…"

"To say what, dammit? What are you trying to avoid saying?"

"No one's told you?" Fiezel temporized.

"Told me *what?*"

"I'm sorry to be the one to have to tell you, but your seat belt was cut."

"What—" Bowden did his best to focus. "What do you mean? It looked fine on preflight."

Fiezel shook his head. "The part where you latch it was fine. It was cut most of the way through, underneath the seat where it goes into the latching mechanism. You wouldn't have seen it unless you crawled up under the seat and pulled it out. It held under normal usage, but couldn't take the deceleration of a crash."

"How…Why would someone do that?"

Fiezel looked at the floor. "Well, I'm no safety inspector, but it looked like sabotage to me."

"And I ask again. Why would someone do that?"

Fiezel winced as he looked up. "You weren't supposed to survive that crash." He shrugged. "Like I said, I'm no safety inspector or whatever you called them in your time, but that whole crash appeared to be an elaborate trap with one sole purpose—to kill you."

Bowden lay back on the bed and chuckled. "A seat belt breaks, and you see murder plots? Are you still seeing VC inside the wires?"

"I wish it were as simple as that," Fiezel said. He cocked his head. "It would make it a whole lot easier." He paused and met Bowden's eyes. "It's not, though."

"What do you mean?"

"Well, after they pulled you from the aircraft, I went and looked at everything, inside and out. Once I saw the seatbelt—which there's no doubt in my mind was cut—I followed the chain of events from start to finish, and there it was."

"There *what* was?"

"The plot to kill you."

"Why don't you start from the beginning? Perhaps the drugs or whatever the local shaman gave me has addled my brain, but I'm not seeing it."

"Okay, from the beginning. You launch, but immediately, your starboard rocket fails. I looked at it; the wire to the rocket was disconnected."

"That could happen on its own. Strange that we didn't see it on preflight or that the ground crew missed it when they were pulling the pin from it."

"We'll come back to that. Next, I looked at the brakes. There were pinhole leaks in the hydraulics to both of the brakes. The leaks wouldn't have manifested until the system was pressurized, but then the hydraulics would have bled out."

"But the right brake worked. At least I think it did."

"It did, but I don't think it was supposed to. I found the hydraulic line still attached to the strut, which came off when the tire blew. The line was holed, but the holes weren't big enough for them to immediately bleed out. Whoever did this messed up. I think you were supposed to drive off the runway and hit something that resulted in a sudden stop, catapulting you—when your seatbelt failed—into the landing gear handle, which would have impaled you right about here." He pointed to his heart. "If not for the fact that the starboard brake still had enough fluid to throw you to the side, you'd be dead right now."

"But why? Who would..."

"Good questions." He shrugged. "It was meant to look like an accident. If I hadn't happened to see the cut seatbelt, I would have thought it was just a series of unfortunate accidents. Why did it happen? I don't know. The 'who,' though; that's a lot easier to figure out. Have you pissed off any of the ground guys? Someone that might want to frag you?"

Bowden shook his head, overwhelmed. "Not that I'm aware of. Who even *does* that?"

Fiezel gave a wry chuckle. "Happened in my era a couple of times. One time a ground maintenance guy got extended when he thought he was going back to The World. Got pissed off and, under the influence of drugs, messed up some of the planes' systems. He wasn't trying to kill anyone; he just wanted to take his frustrations out on the planes and break some stuff. Didn't matter to the guy who did a shitty preflight and took one of those jets flying. He crashed and died. When we found other planes had been sabotaged, we tracked it back to the maintainer. He was sad—and even sadder when he went to Leavenworth for his crimes—but that didn't bring back the pilot who died, who was a friend of mine." He shrugged. "Like I said, it happened sometimes."

"No, I'm not aware that I pissed off anyone or that any of the maintenance guys were mad at anyone or anything. And we *did* a good preflight. We knew about the missing ball from the landing gear handle, but we figured we'd just get a new one when we got up to the habitat."

"That's just it. Whoever did this *knew* the systems. Some of the stuff was insidious. You wouldn't have seen it—the seatbelt was cut underneath the seat where you wouldn't have been able to see it and the brake lines wouldn't have failed until right when you needed them. Not sure how you would have missed the rocket, though…" He pursed his lips. "Who followed who around the plane?"

"What do you mean?"

"Were you following Hrensku around, or did he follow you?"

"As the qualified guy, he followed me."

"So he could have loosened the wire after you checked it."

"But why?"

"No idea. The fact remains, though, that someone—someone who knows the systems in the aircraft really well—took a lot of time and effort to wreck that plane, and to do it in a manner that would kill you without being obvious about it."

"But the cut seatbelt was obvious."

"It sure was." Fiezel nodded. "Here's the thing, though. When I took Sam Hirst out to the wreck to show him and get his opinion on it, the seatbelt was missing from the wreck and the rocket motor wire had been reconnected."

Bowden's jaw dropped as everything became real to him for the first time. "Any chance you were wrong?"

Fiezel shook his head. "I don't think so. I know I saw the wire hanging, and I know the seatbelt was cut. I guess it's possible that all those things just happened to line up...but I doubt it."

"Had Hrensku been out to the plane before you came back with Hirst?"

"I asked around and one of the maintenance guys said he saw Hrensku coming back from the aircraft. Apparently, he left some of his stuff out there when they brought you in."

"Anyone else go out the wreck?"

"A few of the maintenance types, but none of them remember seeing the seatbelt in the cockpit. Hrensku said the same thing when I asked him."

"So he knows you may be onto him."

Fiezel winced. "Yeah, I wish I hadn't asked him, but I did. I'm not much at police work, I guess. If it's him that did it, he at least knows I'm looking into it."

"Well, until we get this figured out, I wouldn't get into an aircraft that he's been around."

"That thought had crossed my mind." Fiezel coughed theatrically. "I think I'm coming down with the R'Bak crud. May not be able to fly for a few days." He shrugged. "Might even take a couple of weeks to get over it, depending on how things turn out."

* * *

Hrensku looked up from the chart he was going over as Bowden walked into the base operations building. "My friend! It is good to see you mobile again."

"Am I?" Bowden asked.

"Mobile? It certainly appears so. You are walking around, which is better than the last time I saw you."

"I wasn't talking about mobility; I was talking about friendship. Am I really your friend, Burg?"

"Yes. Of course you are. Why would you ask that?"

"Because friends don't try to kill friends."

"What do you mean? I didn't try to kill you. You were the one at the controls when we crashed. In fact, it was *you* who told *me* to keep my hands off the controls."

"I did...but I didn't know you had sabotaged the aircraft."

Hrensku's cheeks turned bright red. "*I did not sabotage the aircraft! You will want to take that back right now!*"

Bowden walked up to Hrensku and looked him in the eyes. "You didn't sabotage it? Because it sure looks like you did."

"That is craziness! Why do you even think it was sabotage? This isn't the first time you've seen a rocket bottle fail."

"No, it isn't. It's the first time I've seen pinholes in brake lines and cut seat belts, though."

"I don't know what you're talking about."

"Really? How about the missing knob on the landing gear handle? Without it, it makes a great stake to impale myself on."

"We both saw it. We both looked for it and couldn't find it."

"I'm wondering if we couldn't find it because it was in your pocket. You're the one who wanted to go even though we hadn't found it."

"Because we were going to miss our launch window. You haven't done many launches, but even *you* have to know that."

"It's all very convenient, isn't it?"

"What is convenient? I didn't try to kill you! I was in the same craft with you!"

"Investigators always talk about looking for someone with motive and opportunity. You certainly had the opportunity to cause all the problems…what I don't understand is why? Why would you do that, Burg? What do you have to gain from killing me?"

"That's just it—I don't have *anything* to gain from killing you, especially when I'd be putting my life at risk to do so."

"That might be the best alibi I've ever heard."

"It's not an alibi; *it is the truth!* You ask me why, Bowden, and I ask you the same thing. *Why* would I try to kill you?"

"I don't know."

"Because there *is* no reason. This is all ludicrous. I didn't try to kill you."

Bowden stared into his eyes for a long time, but he couldn't find deceit in them. "Fine," he finally said. "I believe you."

"Good," Hrensku said. "Because you should." He indicated the chart on the table. "Now, can I get back to this? I have a flight in fifteen minutes."

Bowden nodded, turned, and left.

"Did you believe him?" Fiezel asked as he walked out the door. Fiezel had been waiting around the corner, "just in case."

"Yeah," Bowden said. "But that scares me even more than if I didn't believe him."

"Why's that?"

"Because if it *wasn't* Hrensku who sabotaged the plane, who did? And when will he or she strike next?"

* * * * *

Chapter Ten

"So you're now a fully qualified space pilot?" Murphy asked in his office a week later.

"I'm not certified by anyone or anything...but yeah," Bowden said. "I can do launches, fly anywhere you need me to go, and then do a re-entry to a touchdown."

"Good. I was a little worried after your first launch..."

"That wasn't my failure; that was sabotage."

"I know, but I was worried. Anything I need to know about?"

"Like what?"

"Were there any other incidents after that?"

"None. I did three launches, including one with Burg Hrensku; all were nominal. Launches are actually pretty easy if you survive the RATO takeoff. After that, it's just 'keep flying up.' Then the sky gets black, and you go where you need."

Murphy looked toward the hatch. "James?"

A large Terran filled the hatchway in every direction, and Bowden wondered where Max Messina, Murphy's sleepy-eyed bodyguard, had gotten to. He'd rarely seen Murphy without Max nearby, and now this was two times in a row. He wanted to ask about Max but doubted Murphy would tell him if he did.

"Yes, sir?" James asked.

"Could you see that we're not disturbed?"

"Yes, sir. I'll take care of it." He closed the hatch.

Bowden smiled. "Is it game time?"

"Yes, as a matter of fact, it is." He sighed. "Past game time, actually. I would have liked to have given you a few extra days for another launch and re-entry, but we need you now. Needed you yesterday, if you want to know the truth."

"Is that a figure of speech or did you really need me yesterday?"

"I really needed you yesterday. Certain opportunities presented themselves that we needed to grab hold of. Now we're going to be playing catch-up."

Murphy's eyes bored into Bowden's. "Before we go any further, I'm sure you realize this is all strictly classified; I'm the only person with whom you can discuss any of these details with."

Bowden nodded. "Based on your earlier comments, I figured it was something like that. I won't say a word."

"Good, because—as you've seen—there are entities in this system who are not onboard with what we're doing."

"Besides the Kulsians."

"Yes. People closer to home. People who would sabotage an interface craft full of supplies to prevent what we're intending. They'd like to stop our daily operations. If they knew the mission on which I was about to send you…"

"There'd be conflict?"

"They would certainly do their utmost to stop us, even more so than they have thus far. Hopefully, by presenting them with a *fait accompli*, they will have no choice but to join with us."

"Do we know who these forces are?"

"People among the SpinDogs and RockHounds who are far more comfortable hiding from the Kulsians than they are taking the fight to them. They are unhappy with the way we've upset their apple carts."

"Isn't it a little late to try to hide this time around? We've already made our presence known on the planet."

Murphy nodded. "We have, and yes, it's too late to try to hide. That doesn't mean they don't wish it was otherwise."

"Got it. So what's the mission?"

"There is a lighter—a small freighter—going from R'Bak to the second planet in this system where the Kulsians are already harvesting. We have put people in place to capture it. You and a small team of SpinDogs and RockHounds will rendezvous with the lighter—which is already on its way to the second planet, in accordance with its normal profile. I need you to figure out a way to catch up to it, then, once you do, you'll load the two modules of commandos you're carrying onto it."

"Modules?"

"They're transfer boxes, but they look a lot like the CONEX boxes we had back home."

"Who's in charge of the commandos?" Bowden asked.

"It doesn't matter, and you don't need to know. You'll load the transfer boxes—with their cargo—onto the lighter, then you'll do whatever is required to get intercepted by the corvette operating above the second planet. At that point, the commando team you're carrying will capture the corvette for future operations."

"A corvette, eh? That kind of ship would be able to make it to the other system, wouldn't it?" Bowden smiled broadly. "I can see a whole host of future operations that would be possible if we had one of those…"

The smile was lost on Murphy, who frowned. "I would appreciate it if you kept any suppositions of what might be possible in the future to yourself and concentrated on the original mission—getting your team into place."

Bowden's smile faded. "Yes, sir. I understand. Take the lighter to the second planet and get close to the corvette so we can grab it. Who else am I supposed to coordinate with for this?"

"You're coordinating with me. It isn't necessary or desired for you to know or interact with the people you'll be transporting. This is strictly a need-to-know operation, and you don't need to know who the cargo is. The SpinDogs and RockHounds on your team will need to know even less. The commandos are in their own modules, and the only time you'll need to talk to them is when you give them the 'go' code to begin their part of the operation."

"Okay, got it. Don't talk to the commandos." Bowden pursed his lips as he thought, then he shook his head. "I'm sorry, sir, but that's not going to work."

Murphy's eyes hardened. "It's going to work because you're going to make it work."

"Sir, you were involved in a lot of joint operations, right?"

"I was, which is why I know how important doing this under blackout conditions is. We can't give them any indication we're coming. More importantly, if there is a double-agent in one of those modules, we need to deprive them of any information they could use to craft a tailor-made sabotage scheme."

"Sir, a complete comms blackout imposes greater dangers than any possible sabotage, because the most important part of this operation occurs when the *cargo* streams out to capture the corvette. How am I supposed to orient them so that when they come out, they know where to go and what to do? If I don't have a method of communicating with them, their odds of success are going to go way down. Ever have a mission where the recon elements couldn't talk to the operators? And what if we have a critical malfunction? Bottom line: we need the ability to talk to them if required, or at least let them know what's happening."

Murphy cocked his head and was silent for a few moments, then he sighed. "There's a comm panel on one of the transfer boxes. You can jack in there and give them a one-way message."

"What about the guys in the second module?"

Murphy smiled. "Don't worry about it. They can handle their own internal communications. And they are the sabotage risk, anyway."

"Fine," Bowden said, happy to have gotten at least a small concession. "Is there any other information you can give me on the turnover of the lighter?"

"A different team will secure the craft; that's not your problem. You just need to catch up to the craft as soon as you can, and hopefully before it gets to the second planet. At that point, the Kulsians are likely to see it and anyone operating around it. The corvette is armed with ship-to-ship missiles, so you don't want to do anything that will make them shoot first and ask questions later."

"Has any planning gone into how to get them close to us, then?"

"Yes. You will have the proper codes, and you will make it look like there is a problem with your spaceship. The best way is probably to send out a mayday saying you had an impact with something that has put you into a three-axis tumble, and then kill your radio signal.

"Hopefully, that will get them close enough for the commando team to storm across and capture their ship."

"You know that hope isn't a strategy, right, sir?"

"I do, but I have you to fill in all the other operational data to make this happen. We've invested a huge amount of assets in setting this up; I need you to bring it to fruition."

"A three-axis tumble, eh? That's probably something the cargo might want to be aware of before we do it."

"They were pre-briefed to expect that."

"Fair enough." Bowden shrugged. "What happens if we get caught?"

"Don't get caught. I doubt you'd be treated very well by the Kulsians."

"I see." Bowden thought for a moment. "So, failure isn't an option. We either succeed…"

"Or you won't be coming back."

"Got it. The lives of my team, plus the lives of the commandos, are all riding on the success of this mission."

Murphy shook his head. "No, Major Bowden. This mission is much more important than that. If you fail, the Kulsians will become aware of our presence here in the Shex system, and it will provoke a response beyond our ability to stop. The lives of everyone on R'bak as well as the spins and everywhere else will be in jeopardy. If you fail, we stand to lose it all."

"So," mused Bowden, "just like taking out the transmitter last year."

"Yes," Murphy agreed with a very long sigh, "just like that."

* * * * *

Chapter Eleven

Bowden walked into the hangar bay Murphy had mentioned, and his eyes widened to find Burg Hrensku and Malanye Raptis talking to Karas'tan Kamara in front of Kamara's ship, which had two boxy structures—that *did* look very much like CONEX boxes—mounted on top of it. The RockHound nodded to him as he approached, and the others turned to gaze expectantly at him.

"Hi, umm...everyone." When they continued to look at him, he turned to Kamara. "Uh, can I talk to you?"

"It's okay," Kamara replied. "This is the rest of the team."

"Seriously?" Bowden asked, a little louder than was necessary. "Seriously?" he asked in a more conspiratorial tone. "This is just like old home week."

Raptis' brows knit. "What does that mean?"

Bowden smiled. "Nothing. It's just a way of saying everyone's back together again. I've spent more time in space with the three of you than anyone else. Other than Kamara, I didn't know you'd all be part of this, and it surprised me to see you all here."

"It appears that your Murphy called in a number of favors," Raptis said. "With the loss of my ship, I didn't have anything better to do, but Kamara and Hrensku had trips that had to be canceled so they could be part of this."

Bowden scanned the hangar bay; a number of SpinDogs were walking around. "Why don't we go inside the ship to talk?"

The others nodded and followed him into Kamara's ship.

"So, how much do you know about what we're supposed to do?" Bowden asked once they crowded into the ship's small galley area.

"Only that my ship was completely repaired and refurbished for it, at no cost to me, and two modules were brought and attached to it," Kamara said. "What can you tell us?"

"At the moment, I'm not at liberty to tell you anything other than this mission is incredibly dangerous and extremely important, and that I need your assistance to accomplish it. You can read into that whatever you'd like. Once we get to where we're going—or at least are on our way there—I can give you more of the details."

Kamara shook his head. "They want us to follow your directions—to do something you admit is extremely dangerous—and you won't tell us what it is?"

"Sorry," Bowden replied, "I've been sworn to secrecy." His eyes swept across the group. "You can back out now, I guess, if you don't want to be part of this, but I can't give you any more information at this time."

"I, for one, can't back out," Hrensku said. "The Primus asked me to do this as a favor; if I drop out, he will be greatly displeased with me."

"Wouldn't want that," Bowden said with a chuckle.

Hrensku didn't join in the mirth but looked Bowden in the eyes. "No, I wouldn't," he said after a moment. "You have no idea."

"Well, I was told I'd get a new ship of my own at the end of this mission," Raptis said with a bit more humor. "I figured it was going to be something dangerous, but everything I owned was on my old ship. When the comet ate it, it took away my life. This is my chance to start over again."

"If you survive," Kamara said darkly.

Raptis nodded. "If I survive."

Bowden shrugged, and his eyes met Kamara's. "I'm in because Murphy gave me an order, and I believe in this mission. Seems like you're the only one with a choice. Are you in or out?"

Kamara's eyes dropped to the table. He didn't move for a few seconds, but then he sighed and looked back up. "Yes," he said finally. "I am in."

* * *

Bowden checked the hydraulic fluid level and shut the access hatch. After the accident on the planet, his preflight inspections had become *very* thorough. A smiling Dave Fiezel stood waiting when he turned around.

"Any problems?" the former air force officer asked.

"No," Bowden replied. "I haven't found anything that looked like sabotage since that one flight."

"Good." Fiezel winked and nodded to the spacesuit and gear he carried. "Because I'm coming with you."

"You are? Since when did you get qualled to fly in space?"

Fiezel chuckled. "About the same time as you, apparently, but my training was a little more…under the radar, shall we say? I didn't blow up any interface craft or rescue maidens from comets or anything like that." He smiled. "Little did either of us know, but I was your back-up for this…whatever it is."

Bowden felt the blood rush to his cheeks. "In case I got killed? Was I nothing more than bait? Or was it because Murphy didn't think I could cut it?"

"I don't think so," Fiezel said, shaking his head slowly. "I think my training was nothing more than Murphy being cautious. Bad things happen in space, and your trip to the comet could easily have gone horribly wrong. I think I was nothing more than Murphy wanting a backup option. And, with everyone looking at you, I could get my training under the radar."

"Okay," Bowden said, a little mollified. "So why are you here? I've got this."

"Yes you do, and I wouldn't want to take your place." He held up a hand. "Before you ask, I don't know any more than you do about it; in fact, I probably know even less than you do. All I know is that I'm just here to pilot the packet once you get to…wherever it is we're going."

Bowden nodded. "We better get at it, then. We're already behind schedule."

* * *

The packet launched from the habitat, and Bowden had Kamara put it on a flight path to Outpost, then everyone met in the ship's small galley.

"Are you finally going to tell us what we're doing?" Kamara asked.

"Well, I'm going to tell you what I can for now, anyway," Bowden said. "We're trying to catch up with a package that was launched from R'Bak yesterday for the second planet."

Amazement—and a little shock—flew across the SpinDog and RockHounds' faces. Fiezel's remained a neutral mask. Raptis was the first to speak. "A package?" she asked. She cocked her head. "I take it this package is valuable."

Bowden nodded. "Very valuable. And we need its contents."

Hrensku shook his head. "If they see us—either before or after we catch up with the package, the Kulsians will kill us."

"They will," Bowden agreed. "Our first priority is to remain unseen."

Kamara shook his head. "There is nothing in that package important enough for us to risk ourselves and this ship."

"It's more important than that," Hrensku said. "If the Kulsians see us, it is possible they will come search us out and destroy everyone on the spins."

Bowden nodded again. "That's why it's imperative we remain undetected."

"Still," Raptis said, "this is a near-suicide mission."

Bowden shrugged. "And yet, I tell you that it's necessary for not just us Terrans, but the well-being of everyone in the system." He paused and then added. "Anyone that wants to get out at Outpost is welcome to do so."

"I don't have anywhere else to be at the moment," Raptis said. "I'm still in."

"Nothing has changed for me," Hrensku noted. "I imagine the Primus was aware of what this mission entailed when he asked me to come. I doubt he would have done so if this mission wasn't vital."

Kamara nodded slowly. "True...at least to a point, I guess."

"What does that mean?" Fiezel asked.

Kamara raised an eyebrow. "It means you have no idea of how things work here." He shrugged. "As Burg said, though, nothing has changed. I am still in." He shifted to look at Bowden. "If we need to go in-system, though, why are we headed to Outpost?"

Bowden smiled, happy to have at least their partial buy-in. *That's probably going to change, though, once they see what we're really doing.* "Some of you are aware of what I did back before I came here, right?"

"You flew atmospheric fighters from ships on your planet," Hrensku said.

"Correct. On takeoff, though, we only had a hundred meters to achieve flight speed."

"How did you do it? You certainly didn't use RATO on a ship. Or did you?"

Bowden chuckled. "No, we didn't. That would have made things…interesting, to say the least. No, what we used was a catapult system to get us up to speed in the shortest amount of space possible, and that got me thinking…"

"The railgun," Kamara said, catching on. "You want to use Outpost's railgun to get us up to speed."

"Well, I'm not saying I *want* to do it that way, but that's the only way I can think of to give us the velocity we need."

"It won't work," Kamara said.

"Why's that?"

"It's never been done before."

"That doesn't mean it *can't* be done. It just means no one's *needed* to do it before."

"Or been stupid enough to try it," Hrensku noted.

"Or that," Bowden acknowledged. "Having said that, though, I looked at the design of the gun and this ship, and I think it can be done."

Raptis shook her head. "I don't think it will give us enough velocity."

"Especially with whatever those modules that were added have in them," Kamara said. "What's in them?"

"I'm not at liberty to say," Bowden replied. "Not yet, anyway."

"Can you tell me what their mass is, then?"

"Five thousand kilograms."

Kamara shook his head. "The railgun won't give us enough velocity to catch up to your package."

"Well, no," Bowden admitted. "Not on the initial stroke anyway. And not in its current configuration." *Not from what I did with back-of-the-napkin math. A supercomputer would figure this all out easily...if we could use any of the ones we have.* "Let me tell you about baseball."

"What's that?" Raptis asked.

"It's a sport we play back on Earth," Fiezel said. "What's that got to do with it?"

Bowden smiled. "I'm glad you asked. One of the positions is called 'the catcher,' and his job it to catch a ball that's thrown as hard as the person called 'the pitcher' can throw it."

"I don't understand," Raptis said.

"Well, I was thinking about the glove he wears to keep from breaking his hand. It's nice and padded to absorb the force of the ball."

"I still do not understand."

"What would you say if we built something similar on the back of the packet and then, after launch, had the railgun fire several heavy slugs into it, giving us additional velocity?"

"I would say you are doing your best to destroy my ship," Kamara said.

"I don't think so," Bowden replied. "Not if we add a shock absorber system to mitigate the instantaneous shock to the structure of the craft from catching the slugs." *And besides, it's far more likely that the force of the catapult is going to destroy the ship by ripping off your landing gear,* Bowden thought. *Especially since the craft's never been stressed—or intended—for something as stupid as that.*

"That might work," Kamara admitted. "Maybe. It would be better, though, if you used smaller slugs. It would reduce the kinetic shock from each impact and would be easier on both the ship and the crew."

"You're probably right," Bowden allowed. "It would also make it easier to kick the slugs away from your ship if they were smaller." *And less likely to completely destroy us if the system fails or there's a glancing blow to the ship.*

"The downside to using more of the slugs," Bowden continued, "is the error ratio. Whatever the fail rate is on this, the more shots that are fired, the more likely we're going to get one off angle or out of tolerance." He shook his head. "We need something that can increase our accuracy."

"What about if we used some laser targeting for this?" Hrensku asked.

"Laser targeting?"

"Yes. We could place lasers on the ship and on Outpost, and fire them at each other. When the two beams are centered in the others' reception dishes, the system can fire the slugs. That should give the system a higher accuracy rate and reduce the chances of failure."

And take the onus of aiming off the backs of the half-witted local computers, Bowden thought. He nodded. "What do you think?" he asked, looking at Kamara.

Kamara chewed on his lower lip for a moment, then nodded slowly. "It might work."

"Good," Bowden said. "There's one more thing..."

"What?" Kamara asked. "You haven't come up with enough ways to kill us yet?"

"In order for us to be light enough for the railgun to give us enough initial velocity, we're going to have to remove a lot of the craft's cosmic ray shielding."

Hrensku nodded. "You *do* want us to die."

"No, I don't," Bowden said. "But I *do* want us to succeed. To do so, we're going to need to dump a lot of the water that provides the ship's cosmic ray shielding."

"Out of the question," Kamara stated.

"It's not forever," Bowden replied. "I have a plan."

"Of course you do," Raptis said. "Can you share it with us, or are you not at liberty to tell us this, either?"

"The plan is easy. Before we launch, we use the railgun to fire several pods down our line of travel at a slower velocity than we'll be traveling. As we pass them, we scoop them up. Then, once we are safely away from Outpost, the railgun can go back to its normal operation of shooting pods, except it will be shooting pods to us that are full of the rest of the water and fuel we'll need for the mission, and we can replenish them en route. Since the pods don't have passengers, they could be launched by the railgun at extremely high gees."

"You're really serious about this," Kamara said.

"I am," Bowden replied. "It does two things for us. Not only does it allow the mass of the ship to be extremely light at launch, but it doesn't increase our total signature. Each of the supply containers can be kept relatively small and made of lightweight materials that will be extremely difficult to detect."

Raptis shook her head. "There's only one problem with all that."

"What's that?"

"Who's going to go out and capture all these pods? You?"

"Don't worry about it," Bowden replied. "The cargo will handle the acquisition and retrieval of the supply pods."

"*The cargo?*" Raptis asked. "You mean there are *people* in those boxes?"

"Yes, there are, and yes, they are trained in EVA operations. They are coming to help recover the package we are going after; they can bring the supply pods aboard and pump the additional water and fuel into the tanks. We'll need to stay in a relatively small area of the ship at the start, but as more and more of the water is brought aboard, we'll have full access to the entire ship."

Bowden looked at the faces of the crew and saw a mixture of disbelief. "Okay, I don't like it any more than you do, and I know it makes you put a lot of trust into people you don't know really well, but I am here to tell you that they can, *and they will*, get it done."

"Are you willing to bet your life on this?" Hrensku asked.

It's gotta be Tapper, and if I can't trust him, who can I trust? Bowden nodded. "I already am."

Hrensku sighed. "Then I will as well."

"I'm in, too," Fiezel said quickly.

"I'm too much of a mercenary to give up the chance to get a ship out of this," Raptis added. "I am in."

Everyone looked at Kamara. After a few seconds, he jerked his head in a single nod. "Against my better judgment, I—and my ship—are in, too."

Bowden nodded back. "Outstanding. We're pressed for time on this, so we need to get everything in place as soon as possible."

The meeting broke up immediately after, with Kamara, Raptis, and Hrensku going to see what Kamara had that could be used for the 'catcher's mitt' and the laser targeting system. Fiezel stayed and pursed his lips. "Were you really going to let them leave at Outpost if they weren't onboard with the mission?" he asked in a whisper.

Bowden shook his head. "Think Murphy would have allowed that?"

"No. What were you going to do if someone had wanted to get off?"

Bowden shrugged. "Whatever it took to stop them or convince them to continue." *Including using the pistol that's in my gear if it had proven necessary. Happily it wasn't...this time.*

* * * * *

Chapter Twelve

"We are ready," Kamara transmitted from the pilot's seat. He turned his helmeted head to look at Bowden in the co-pilot's position. "I hope this works."

Me too. "It should," Bowden said. "Attaching it directly to the rear of the fuselage and at the center of mass lets the main structural members absorb the force of the acceleration." He'd had to figure out another way to do it after looking at the nose gear of the packet again. The ship—in general—was on the spindly side, and there was no way the nose gear would have survived the railgun launch. The fuselage was marginally sturdier, assuming the mounted CONEX boxes didn't tear off.

He clicked the mic twice to let the commandos know of the impending launch. *The railgun ride was going to provide a lot of 'fun' for the commandos.* During the installation of the catcher's mitt, he'd had a wire attached to the command CONEX box that led to the bridge of the ship. Then, when he'd had a few unobserved minutes, he'd passed the word to them about the launch so that they knew to be lying down so they wouldn't get hurt. He'd also told them about the plan to use them to go EVA and get the fuel/water fired from the railgun. They hadn't come running out of the boxes in disapproval, so Bowden figured that their silence gave their consent, and that they'd do it. *Or everyone was probably going to die on the mission.*

There was a pause as the SpinDog inside Outpost waited for the railgun to get to its optimal position, then, without another transmission, he pushed the button—or however he initiated the railgun launch system—and the ship was hurled from the station. "Hurled" probably wasn't the right word, as the forces involved weren't as violent as an aircraft carrier catapult launch, but it certainly induced more stress than the packet was designed for.

The sounds of metal under stress filled the cockpit, and a number of caution lights illuminated on the packet's dashboard, but none of the red warning lights illuminated. After a few seconds, the acceleration fell off, and Bowden began breathing again. *It worked!*

"Well, we're still alive and in once piece," Kamara said as his fingers pushed several reset buttons. Most—but not all—of the caution lights went out. "I even think we can fix most of the failures you induced—"

"But?" Bowden asked when Kamara left the statement dangling.

"But now we will see what happens when the gun shoots thousand-kilogram slugs at my poor ship."

While Bowden hadn't been oblivious to the dangers inherent to his plan, his scheme to catch the slugs hadn't sounded quite so dangerous until it was phrased like that. "It'll work," he said simply.

Or people will die as giant bits of metal rip through the impromptu mechanism and crash through the ship. Bowden swallowed. *Please, dear God, let this work.*

"Are we good?" Kamara asked.

"As good as we're going to be," Raptis said as she monitored the catching mechanism from her position in the back. "The glove is aligned."

"We are ready," Kamara reported to Outpost.

"Firing," the man replied.

A few seconds later, the craft jerked forward as the glove sequentially caught and then dumped the first six slugs the system on Outpost fired.

"It worked!" Kamara exclaimed, surprise evident in his tone, as the mitt rotated to the side to dump the last of the slugs out of the way and re-aligned for the next round.

Those were the easy ones, Bowden thought. By the time Outpost rotated into position again, they would be a lot farther from the station, making the shot more difficult. A good computer system could have made the shot from the spinning platform...but they only had the jury-rigged laser system. "Hopefully, they can do that six more times," he said.

And hopefully, the rockets will work, too. A set of discrete solid rocket boosters had been added to the rest of the slugs. It gave the rounds a little more velocity and a limited terminal correction capability— including the ability to abort the round if there was a malfunction that would lead to an impact outside the mitt.

"The glove is aligned for the second set of shots," Raptis said, having confirmed the mechanism was secured in its "catch" position.

"Ready," Kamara transmitted.

"Firing."

The technician at Outpost was on the money with the first several shots of the next group, but, on the fourth, Bowden felt a brief moment of acceleration and then *slam!*

"What was that?" Kamara asked as a number of caution lights illuminated. This time, some of the red warning lights illuminated, too.

"The camera is out, so I can't see," Raptis said, "but from the brief glimpse I got, it looked like the fourth round tried to abort. It turned a catastrophic hit into a glancing blow, but the slug still hit the ship."

"Shit," Kamara said, pushing the button that jettisoned the device they'd been using to catch the slugs. He pointed to one of the red lights. "It looks like it must have hit the port aft thruster. I'm going to have to go out and check it."

"What do you want me to do?" Bowden asked.

"We didn't get enough velocity to get to the second planet," the RockHound said, "but we got too much to return to Outpost. I need you and Raptis to figure out where we can go from here without being seen by the Kulsians."

* * *

"The good news," Kamara said when he came back in two hours later, "is that I can fix the thruster. I have a spare and—with a bit of work by Hrensku and me—we can fix it and a couple of other problems the slug caused. I also just saw some of the water in the shielding being replenished, so our cargo has obviously picked up the first pod, and the system is working. The bad news, however, is that we're not going to be able to rendezvous with the package without using a good bit of thrust—so much that the thrust signature is sure to be detected, and none of us want that to happen."

Kamara looked around the small group gathered in the galley. "The worse news, of course, is that we're headed further in-system without a way to return to Outpost without a similar thrust signature, which would be sure to bring the Kulsians to investigate. I don't see any way for us to get home or to accomplish the fool's errand we were on."

"I thought the same thing," Raptis said, "but then Bowden had an idea."

"Is this one going to be as good as your catcher's mitt idea, which worked out *so* well?" Kamara asked. "Or is it something equally dangerous and unpredictable?"

Bowden shrugged. "It's not without risks, but—like you said—we're pretty much out of options."

"And this plan is?"

"Well, the problem, as you articulated, is that whatever we do, we have to do it without being seen."

"Correct. Leading the Kulsians to Outpost would result in the destruction of our society."

Bowden nodded. "As you also articulated, though, we're not going to make it to our rendezvous without using additional thrust. That means, we need to have a burn, but we have to do it without the Kulsians seeing it."

"And the closer we get, the more likely they are to see it, so if you could just explain your plan…"

"Right. Remember when we were on the comet together?"

"Yes, but I don't see how that's going to help us."

"Bear with me. Remember how it was outgassing?"

"Yes."

"That would hide our thrust bloom if we did it on the other side of a comet from the planet, but we'd need to be very close to the comet."

"And there is a comet we could use to hide our signature?"

"Well, yes," Bowden said. Raptis raised an eyebrow. "Okay, there's an ice-teroid headed inbound, but it isn't currently outgassing."

"An ice-teroid isn't a comet. It's just a conglomeration of rock and ice. It doesn't have the outgassing we need. How does that help us?"

"The formation of comets and such isn't uniform. Just because it isn't outgassing yet just means the star hasn't shed enough light on it to raise the temperature to the point at which the outgassing process begins. I'm suggesting we rendezvous with it and focus our thrusters on it to get an outgassing event, then we use it to conceal our thrust as we boost for the system."

Kamara shook his head once as he thought it through, then looked up at Raptis. "You're the expert; what do you think?"

"I think it's our only chance. Just because it's not outgassing doesn't mean it won't. I've been to dozens of comets and a number of these have had their surface ice melted off, which takes them a while to heat up enough to get the ice inside to melt off. Ice-teroids are similar...somewhat. It's possible we can do this, but we won't know until we get there and take a look."

"Where is 'there?'"

Raptis winced. "The ice-teroid is still behind us, but it's catching up quickly. We would have to start accelerating soon to match its velocity as it overhauls us."

"Won't we be seen by the Kulsians if we do that?" Fiezel asked.

"No," Raptis said. "We can use the compressed gas thrusters to speed up without tapping the main engine. I think it's possible. Once we're in the shadow of the comet, we could tap the main engine once or twice if we needed to."

"It might work," Hrensku said. "If one of the Surveyor ships came over the horizon and was looking our way, they wouldn't see the thrust signature; all they'd get would be a heated particle trail. Something that would be easily passed off as comet outgassing."

"I've never thought about using one for cover that way," Kamara admitted. "It's risky, especially with Kulsians close by. Normally, we'd just snuggle up to it, go quiet, and try to hide behind it. I mean, who'd be *dumb* enough to try to get a body to outgas while you're flying in formation with it? I mean, the material spewing forth could potentially destroy the craft as easily as a Kulsian ship-to-ship missile."

"That's the greatest risk," Raptis agreed. "We're going to have to get *really* close because we're going to have to use the main engine to create the heat we need. It's going to take focusing the burn down onto the ice-teroid while using the forward thrusters at full throttle to match and counteract the main engine, maintaining our station keeping. Then, once it's going like we want, we spin the ship and use a few heavy pulses of main thrust."

"But you think it's possible?" Kamara asked.

"I never would have thought of it on my own," she said. "But I think it could work. If we can find the right area on the ice-teroid. Besides, we don't have any other choices."

"You're right." Kamara shrugged. "We can't make it back to Outpost without being seen, so I don't see how we can do anything else. A small chance of success is better than none at all."

* * * * *

Chapter Thirteen

"**A**nd...*now!*" Raptis exclaimed as the packet slid into the ice-teroid's shadow.

Kamara gave the ship a small boost to match the ice-teroid's velocity. A fairly large body, the object was pear shaped, nearly sixteen kilometers long and ten kilometers in diameter at its widest point. The thin end, which pointed generally away from the star as it slowly tumbled through space, was only about six kilometers.

"Okay," Kamara said when he was satisfied with the craft's positioning alongside the narrow end. His shoulders sagged as he released the breath he'd been holding. He turned to Raptis. "Your turn."

Raptis nodded and pushed off toward the airlock. "Come on, Bowden. This was your idea. You're my back up."

* * *

"**W**e got lucky," Raptis announced once she and Bowden returned from their spacewalk two hours later. "There's a vein not too far up from this end. It's big, but the fatter end of the asteroid has blocked the seam from being heated too much prior. There is a lot of ice inside it we can use to our benefit. Because of the way the asteroid is shaped, we can burn our engine without any liminal heat being seen by the planet."

"You're sure you want to do this?" Kamara asked. "There is a possibility that this could go horribly wrong. If something outgasses and hits the ship, we could find ourselves on a vector where no one will ever be able to get us."

Hrensku shrugged. "No one's going to come and rescue us in any event."

"Why's that?" Fiezel asked.

"There's no way they could get to us and get back without being seen," Hrensku said, shaking his head. "And since they can't…"

"They won't," Bowden finished. Hrensku nodded. "Therefore," Bowden continued, "it's up to us, and this is the only way we're going to get there without being seen. We have to try it. If it doesn't work or we're seen doing it, then we'll have to come up with a different plan."

"What would that be?" Kamara asked.

"I have no idea, so let's just make this work. Okay?"

Raptis chuckled. "It's our only hope, and the ice seam looked good. I say we try it."

"I agree," Hrensku said. "It really is our only chance of completing the mission…which is our only chance of getting out of this alive."

"I'm in," Fiezel said.

"As am I," Kamara said. "Anything is better than being caught by the Kulsians." He shrugged. "Even drifting off into space with no chance of rescue."

As complicated as the maneuver was going to be—to put them on a vector that would pull them into an orbit around the second planet without anything other than minor thruster corrections—Kamara booted up the computer, and they worked out the vector and thrust they'd need to intercept the planet. The results had Kamara shaking his head.

"It's going to take a big thrust pulse to get us there, which means that not only are we going to need a big outgassing screen to hide behind, we're also going to have to start our thrust for the planet much closer to the asteroid so we're not seen."

"It's what we have to do," Bowden said, "so let's do it. You take the pilot's seat, and I'll back you up as co-pilot."

"Very well. Everyone else is going to need to be strapped in. There is no telling what will outgas from the asteroid, nor where it will go when it does."

"Everyone's ready," Bowden said a little while later, once the packet—and the people onboard—were as secure as possible. Bowden had also passed the word to the commandos in the modules to secure themselves for thrust/collision; both outcomes were possible with what they were planning.

"Maneuvering," Kamara said. The ship was pointed away from the asteroid, and he walked it over sideways with the ACS thrusters, using the cameras at the back of the craft to watch his progress.

Bowden forced himself to breathe as the landscape of the asteroid passed beneath him far closer than he was comfortable with. After a few minutes, the seam appeared below them, darker in color than the rocky surface, and Kamara used the attitude control system thrusters again to stabilize their position over it.

"Here we go," Kamara said. Bowden could hear the strain in the pilot's voice as he intentionally put his ship—and everyone onboard—in danger. His fingers danced as he slowly advanced power to the engine while matching it with the ACS system to hold his position.

Nothing happened.

"We need to move closer," Kamara said.

"Give it a minute," Bowden replied. "Let it heat."

"We won't have the fuel for an extended burn if we waste it playing with this."

Bowden's eyes darted to the fuel gauge. The level was dropping—slowly, but visibly—toward the mark Kamara had drawn. When it reached the mark, they had to boost for the planet or they wouldn't have the fuel to reach it.

"Okay," Bowden agreed. "A little closer."

"Moving," Kamara said. He reduced thrust ever so slightly, and the ship moved toward the asteroid. Within seconds, vapor began to boil away from the ice seam.

"It's working," Bowden said.

"See, we just needed to get—" Without warning, the motor cut out completely, and the asteroid began growing quickly in the camera view. Kamara flipped the switches to restart the engine, but Bowden could see they were going to hit before the engine would be able to develop enough thrust to boost them away.

"Shit!" Bowden said, having had more than his share of bad rendezvous with asteroids. He slapped the aft ACS thrusters to full and killed the forward thrusters, which were pushing them toward the asteroid. The planet continued to grow in the camera view for another few seconds, then—just as it seemed Bowden could reach through the camera and touch the surface—it began to recede again. Bowden jockeyed the ACS controls to slow their velocity away from the planet, then stabilized the ship's position with respect to the asteroid beneath them.

"What the hell was that?" Bowden asked.

"I don't know," Kamara replied. "You saw—the engine just cut out."

"Yeah, but then you didn't do anything to stop our momentum down."

"I was trying to get the motor started."

"We were going to hit. I saved us."

"Maybe," Kamara finally allowed. "Maybe I panicked; I don't know. I thought I could get it restarted in time, but, thinking about it now, maybe not."

"Maybe we should stop and check it," Bowden said.

"No, the fuel we use isn't perfect, and the engine cuts out every once in a while. Let me run the diagnostics on the engine, and we can try again. We're already in position, and I don't want to lose any heating of the ice below that we've already done. We won't have enough fuel if we do."

Kamara restarted the engine and ran the diagnostic on it while Bowden let everyone know what was happening.

"We're ready for another try," Kamara said. "Everything is good, and I can't find anything wrong with the engine. It must have been a bit of bad fuel, as I suspected."

"Okay," Bowden replied, trying to keep his tone level. A second attempt violated most of the procedures he'd learned in the Navy.

"Here we go." Kamara moved the ship closer to the asteroid and increased power.

Bowden leaned forward and kept his hands close to the thruster panel. If it was needed again, he was going to be ready. Having done it once, Kamara moved to the position where they'd been when the motor failed and brought up the power levels again. Within seconds, the ice began to vaporize again, and the cloud of vapor grew quickly. Soon, pieces of rock and other, non-vaporized things began to spew from the crevasse, and Bowden heard a loud *bang!* as one of them hit the hull.

"Want to move a little further from the asteroid?" Bowden asked nervously. A rock that destroyed something in the propulsion system was just as good a mission kill as a Kulsian ship-to-ship missile.

"I've got it," Kamara said, jockeying the craft to the side slightly. The surface of the craft rang with repeated small impacts, almost as if it were raining on the hull.

Bowden glanced up, and his jaw fell. Kamara had a giant smile on his face that could be seen through his helmet as he worked the craft back and forth over the seam. When it got too hard to see the surface, he'd move slowly to the side until he could see again, slowly painting the craft's exhaust over a greater and greater swath of the ice vein.

Smash!

Something spewing forth from the vein hit the camera. There was a flash of rock, then the screen went black. Bowden's finger moved to the ACS thruster.

"No!" Kamara ordered. He looked out the ship's small canopy. "I've still got it. I can see…well enough. I think."

The qualifier didn't do Bowden's nerves any good as the rate of things hitting the hull continued to grow. Bowden would have hated to be the commandos—their boxes were probably taking a pounding and they'd have no idea what was going on. *The container walls are thick—they won't get holed…I hope.* The first yellow warning light illuminated on the control panel. A sensor on the aft portion of the ship had ceased reporting.

Bowden took a quick look out the canopy. He didn't see how Kamara was able to continue. The cloud completely enveloped them, and it continued to grow and thicken. As did the pattern of impacts with the hull.

"How much more can the ship take?" Bowden asked.

"As much as it needs," Kamara replied with a grunt as he slid it back to the right again.

Another glance to the fuel gauge; they were almost at minimum fuel for their maneuver. "The fuel…" Bowden warned.

"I know," Kamara replied.

"You're going to shave it too thin!"

"I know!" He paused, nodded a couple times to himself, then stabbed the enable button on the autopilot. The ACS thrusters cut off and the engine roared to full power. The ship accelerated a second, then spun to its intended course while the engine continued at full thrust. After about ten seconds, it cut out, and Kamara turned to look at him as they started to draw ahead of the ice-teroid as they angled off to the side.

"We're on our way," he said. "For better or worse, we're on our way."

* * * * *

Chapter Fourteen

On the second day outbound from the asteroid, Bowden called the team together. So far, there hadn't been a response to their maneuver from the second planet or any indication that they'd been seen. Passive sensors showed the corvette orbiting the planet as if nothing had happened. Whether that was because the corvette's crew and the planetside operators hadn't seen them or they were just waiting for the packet to get closer, though, no one knew. Bowden, however, had more immediate concerns.

He met each of the team's eyes, but none of them had what he was looking for. Fear of being caught. A dare to be challenged. Not knowing how to proceed, he took a deep breath and just said it. "One of you is a traitor."

"What?" Kamara said. "How do you know someone is a traitor?"

"I looked at the ship's log. The engine dying while we were maneuvering near the asteroid wasn't an accident. Someone programmed it to shut down."

Bowden shook his head. "And this isn't the first time it's happened. Someone sabotaged an interface craft I was flying a few months ago." He looked at Hrensku. "It almost killed me."

"That wasn't me," Hrensku replied. "I didn't do it then, and I didn't do this, either."

"Funny that you were in close proximity to both, though, isn't it?"

"I don't find it funny at all," Kamara said. "I find it horrific. There's only one penalty for such a crime in our society."

"And what's that?" Bowden asked.

"We space him."

"Wait a minute," Hrensku said. "I didn't do either of those things. Why would I make a craft that I was in crash into an asteroid to highlight myself to the enemy? It makes no sense!"

"To make yourself look innocent," Kamara said. "Just like you said. Who would be dumb enough to disconnect a RATO bottle on takeoff?" He shrugged. "And, as to highlighting us, perhaps it is part of a plan for you to curry favor with the Kulsians."

Hrensku turned to Bowden. "I thought you said you believed I wasn't responsible for the crash."

"I do, actually. I believed it at the time, and I believe it now."

"Then who is responsible for this?" Raptis asked.

"I don't know," Bowden replied, "but it has to be one of you RockHounds."

"It isn't me," Raptis said. "What would I stand to gain?"

"A reward?" Hrensku asked. "Perhaps a new ship?"

"But I was promised a new ship when we returned."

Hrensku shrugged. "*If* we returned, you would get it. Maybe you weren't sure we we'd make it, and you were trying to hedge your bets or get in good with the Kulsians."

Raptis turned to Bowden. "You saved my life. I *owe* you. I owe Kamara, too. Our society doesn't dismiss an honor debt so quickly."

"But—in a similar vein—Kamara owes both you and me for saving his life. If that's true, then he didn't do it, either, and we're back where we started."

"Exactly," Kamara said. "Either Hrensku did it, or one of you Terrans did."

"It wasn't me," Bowden said. "I have nothing to gain. If we get caught, I'm looking at a lot of torture, not a reward from the Kulsians. Fiezel would get the same treatment."

Kamara nodded. "Which, once again, leads us back to Hrensku."

"Who I don't think did it."

"Maybe," Raptis said. She shrugged. "And maybe not. Only one person is here voluntarily." She turned to Kamara. "You. Bowden and Fiezel were ordered here, as was Hrensku, for all intents and purposes. I lost my ship; I had nowhere else to go. But you—" she pointed, "—*you* volunteered your ship and your services. Why did you do that? I've never known you to put your life at risk without a large gain."

"I saved your life, didn't I?"

"I suspect that had Bowden not been with you, you would have let me perish, then swooped in to take my ship for your own. That was probably your plan all along. You just happened to show up at the comet in time to rescue me? I'll bet you hoped to find me dead already so you could take my ship and the load it carried. Too bad I wasn't quite dead yet."

"What do you mean? That's crazy! Murphy told me to train him in the worst environments I could. That, to me, means flying near a comet."

Raptis turned to Bowden. "I never told anyone, but my ship was sabotaged. When I landed on the comet and shut down the motor, the fuel lines crimped, and I was unable to start it again. I could have avoided the outgassing—I saw it coming—but my ship wouldn't start up again. I told him—" she nodded to Kamara, "—about an hour before I left that I was headed to the comet."

"An hour prior," Kamara agreed. "There wasn't time for me to do anything to your packet. And it's a good thing you told me about the comet—that's how I knew it existed. If you hadn't told me, you'd be dead now."

"Hmm…" Hrensku said. "I believe I have another perspective on this. On the day of our plane crash, I saw Kamara on the planet. I thought it strange for a RockHound to be planetside, but, in the confusion after the crash, I never got a chance to talk to him, and I never thought about it again. What were you doing there, Kamara?"

"I was down trading for needed supplies," Kamara replied. "It happens. You know RockHounds go to the planet once in a while for supplies."

"Is that true?" Bowden asked.

"Once in a very long while," Hrensku replied. "It isn't unheard of, but it is *very* unusual. Most can't stand the gravity."

"But not unheard of," Kamara said with a nod. "And that is what happened—I was there trading."

"You told me you were on Outpost then," Raptis said.

"I went there after my trip to the planet," Kamara said with a smile. "When I saw you, I was coming from Outpost."

"No." Raptis shook her head. "The numbers don't match. There is no way you could have gotten from the planet, to Outpost, and back in the time you had." She looked to Bowden while pointing at Kamara. "There's your traitor!"

"Wait a minute!" Kamara said. "Just because she says—"

"No," Bowden said, "she's right. You're the traitor."

"What do you mean? I never—"

"Let me ask you one question. How did you know the RATO bottle was disconnected?"

"Well, uh." Kamara sputtered a few seconds, then said, "It was common knowledge that's what happened."

Bowden shook his head. "Fiezel was the one who saw the bottle was disconnected and—as far as I know—he never told anyone." Fiezel shook his head. "I never mentioned it."

"Wait!" Hrensku exclaimed. "The bottle was disconnected?"

Bowden looked at Hrensku to gauge his reaction. "It was."

Hrensku launched himself at Kamara, who tried to block him and force him away. Hrensku bounced off the RockHound but got a handful of Kamara's suit and pulled himself back in. Kamara lost his handhold and the two floated free as they struggled to gain an advantage on each other.

"Stop it!" Raptis exclaimed in a voice that cut through their struggle. "Stop it *right now*."

All four men looked to find Raptis holding a small pistol, which she pointed at Kamara. Hrensku pushed away from the RockHound, and they floated toward opposite bulkheads.

"Why did you do it, Karas'tan?" Raptis asked.

Drops of blood floated free from Kamara's nose. The larger Hrensku had obviously scored on at least one of his blows. Kamara shrugged. "To stop all of this—" he waved a hand around at the lighter, "—as you *know* nothing good can come of it. You know that's true, don't you?"

Raptis shrugged. "I don't know what the plan is, but it's too late to stop it. All we can do now is try to guide it to a successful end." She stared at him a moment. "But you didn't know what we were doing before you came aboard. What is the real reason?"

"Money, of course." Kamara laughed. "People wanted Hrensku dead, and I was sent to kill him."

"Wait," Bowden said. "The RATO sabotage *was* you, wasn't it?"

"Of course. And, if Hrensku had been good enough to sit in the left seat, like he was supposed to, I wouldn't be here now." He chuckled. "You Terrans, always thinking everything is about you." He stared at Bowden for a moment and then added, "It's not."

Hrensku tensed, balling his fists again.

"Stay away from him," Raptis said. "He's told us all we need to know. He's guilty of sabotage and attempted murder."

"You wouldn't," Kamara said. "After I rescued you from the comet?"

"Wouldn't what?" Bowden asked.

"Put him out the airlock," Raptis replied, never taking her eyes off Kamara. "And yes, I would. You may have saved me from the comet, but I saved you and then Bowden saved us both. And you do not gain the Death Fathers' approval for coming to the asteroid since all you *really* wanted to do was kill me and take my goods as your prize."

Kamara shrugged. "It was worth an effort."

"Move!" Raptis ordered. She motioned with the pistol. "Airlock. Now." She shepherded him to the airlock, with the rest of the team in trail. "Strip."

Kamara gave her a cruel smile. "You'd like that, wouldn't you? A chance to see me naked one more time?"

"I couldn't care less about seeing you naked; I just don't want to waste the material in your suit and clothes. They're worth more than the hundred kilos of shit stuffed inside them."

"And if I don't?"

"Then I shoot you, and we toss your bleeding body into the airlock. It'd be a waste of clothes and a pain in the ass to clean up the mess, but it'd be totally worth it. Please, *please,* give me a reason to shoot you."

Kamara slowly peeled away the suit then floated naked in front of Raptis with his arms out to the sides. She shook her head. "Do I have to tell you to do it?"

He nodded. "Yes." He shrugged. "And you'll be sorry if you do."

"What the hell is that supposed to mean?"

"You want me alive. You need me alive."

"You're wrong." Raptis shook her head. "We need you dead. Get in the airlock."

"You'll be sorry."

"I'm already sorry. Now *get in the damned airlock!*"

Kamara opened the airlock door and moved inside, then he turned and looked expectantly at her.

"If you think I'm coming any closer to you so that you can grab me, you're even dumber than I know you are." She motioned toward the door controls. "Shut it."

Kamara pushed the button and moved away from the panel. As the door closed, Raptis suddenly pushed off toward the airlock controls. Seeing her movement, Kamara tried to reverse his direction and beat her to the panel, but she was too fast. She knocked his hand back into the airlock, the door closed, and she cycled the airlock. His scream was lost as the air was ripped from his lungs and his bowels evacuated.

Bowden looked away, having seen enough.

After a few seconds, Raptis cycled the airlock controls. "There was a point in time where he wasn't such a bad guy." She sighed. "Unfortunately, that was a long time ago."

"What do we do now?" Hrensku asked.

"Nothing's changed," Bowden replied. "We're committed and don't have a way to change our vector without being seen. We continue."

* * * * *

Chapter Fifteen

"That's no package!" Raptis exclaimed as the lighter came into view the next day. "That's a Kulsian ship! I had one go past an asteroid I was hiding on a few months ago. Shouldn't we either be running or hiding?" her head whipped from side to side as she scanned everyone's faces. "*That's a Kulsian ship!*"

Bowden shook his head. "No. That's the ship we're meeting up with."

Hrensku turned away from the view screen with what appeared to be a significant effort of will. "Since Malanye seems too stunned to think, I'll ask the obvious question. What, exactly, are we doing rendezvousing with a Kulsian ship?"

Bowden smiled. "It's not a Kulsian ship. Not anymore."

"What?" Hrensku asked. "Are they traitors, too?"

"No, a Terran group captured it."

"You *captured* it? *Are you Terrans out of your minds?*"

"Murphy has a plan."

"I think it's about time you shared this plan with the rest of us," Raptis said, "because—like Hrensku—I can't see how this will lead to anything but the annihilation of our society, and I doubt *any* of us would have come on this mission if we'd known what it was really about."

Bowden shrugged. "I can't tell you about it because I don't know what it is, either. I do, however, know there *is* one, and our mission

129

advances it." Raptis and Hrensku shook their heads, although Bowden was unable to tell whether from fear, disbelief, or some other emotion. Or, maybe, all of them.

"I still need the ship I was promised," Raptis said. She shook her head and sighed. "Despite the fact that I'll probably never see it, I'm still in."

"Me, too," Hrensku said with a sigh. "When the Primus asks…" He shrugged. "We also may be able to help keep things from falling totally apart. You're an okay space pilot, but I'm better. So's Raptis. Besides, I doubt you've ever flown anything that big."

"No, I haven't," Bowden said. "Have you?"

"None of us have," Raptis said. "While the SpinDogs *do* have ships as large as the lighter, those larger hulls are rare, and probably less than ten percent of their pilots have any experience with them. RockHounds have none. Still, though, we have a lot more time in space than you do and can probably understand the scope of flying it better than you."

"That's possible," Bowden allowed. He nodded to the ship on the viewer. "If we're all done discussing it, Malanye, would you do the honors and take us in?"

"Sure," she said. "One question first, though."

"Yeah?"

"What are we going to do with this packet? Kamara isn't going to have any use for it."

"Fiezel was supposed to fly it back, but now we don't have enough fuel to do so," Bowden said. "We could just let it go—"

"No," Raptis said. "It's a significant investment of resources, and it would be a shame to just throw it away. In fact, I know someone who could use a new ship, even one that's had a rock storm beat on its aft end."

"We can't leave it attached to the lighter," Bowden said. "It would compromise the rest of the mission."

"I think it's time you told us what you know," Hrensku said. "I know you don't know it all, but you need to tell us what you do. The traitor is gone, and we've already pledged to help you, but we can't help if we don't know what we're supposed to be trying to accomplish. What is our mission? Better yet, what's really in the modules we're carrying?"

Bowden sighed, looking at the deck, then looked up to meet Hrensku's eyes. "Commandos," he said simply. "The two modules have commandos in them."

Raptis' brows knit. "I thought you said you already controlled the lighter."

"I did, and I hope we do." He shrugged. "We'll have to confirm before we go aboard. If we don't, the commandos will get us aboard the lighter, but that wasn't their intended mission."

"Stop stalling," Hrensku said. "What *is* their intended mission?"

"We are supposed to board the lighter and get the corvette that is in orbit to come close. Then the commandos will go across and capture the corvette."

"*What?*" Hrensku and Raptis chorused. Both looked like they wanted to say something else, but neither were able to articulate their thoughts.

Fiezel chuckled. "We're not known for thinking small, I guess."

"No," Bowden agreed. "We're not." He shrugged. "That's the plan, or as much of it as I know. After we capture the corvette, we'll be given further orders, but I don't know what they'll be, and Murphy wasn't a fan of me speculating on them." He gave them a half smile. "Still with me?"

Hrensku shook his head. "If I could leave, I would, and I'd happily live in hiding from the Primus for the rest of my days. I can't, though, so I'm in."

"You could go with the packet—whatever we determine we're going to do with it."

"I could, but you're more likely to be successful if I stay. As the future of my people rests on the success of this mission, I will stay and help."

"As will I," Raptis said.

"Which leads us back to the question of, what do we do with this packet."

"Is there—" Raptis started, but the engine fired, cutting her off.

Raptis, Hrensku, and Fiezel were thrown to the back of the cockpit. Bowden, seated in the pilot's chair, was barely able to keep his seat. As the Gs mounted, he struggled to turn his seat to face forward, then used it to reach forward and push the Emergency stop button. The engine immediately cut off, and Bowden hit the ACS thrusters to kill the new velocity the engine had given the craft as the lighter grew quickly in the canopy.

The reverse thrust threw the rest of the crew back into the cockpit.

After a few seconds, Bowden had the ship stabilized again with respect to the lighter, and the crew righted themselves again in the zero G.

"The fuck was that?" Fiezel asked.

"Apparently, our traitor wasn't done with us," Bowden said. "He must have left that command in the autopilot. That's what Kamara meant when he said we'd be sorry if we spaced him."

"Asshole," Fiezel said, rubbing an elbow. He nodded to the instrument panel. "Now I don't have enough fuel to do much of anything."

Bowden shook his head slowly as Raptis and Hrensku moved to where they could see. "No," he said, "you don't. We'll have to figure something else out."

* * *

"So, is there a moon to hide behind?" Fiezel asked. "Something like that?"

"No," Raptis said. She'd been tasked with surveying the planet and its environs to search for a good place to hide the packet as the craft approached the lighter. So far, the crew of the ship had given no indication they knew the packet was there despite their last burn. Raptis paused and swiped her tablet. "But there is…what I think is a Kulsian fuel depot in orbit."

"A what?" Fiezel asked, as if he were a man in the desert, dying of thirst, who had just been handed a glass of water. "Really?"

"Really. They probably put it there so they wouldn't have to make planetfall every time." She shrugged. "It's in a medium orbit that would be easy to reach both ways."

"The packet can easily hide there after refueling," Hrensku said, warming to the subject. "That way, there's no exit signature to tip off the Kulsians since it won't leave until the rest of the operation is over. The corvette is too close to boost without being spotted."

134 | CHRIS KENNEDY

"Also, if the mission is a success," Raptis added, "the packet won't have to boost at all. It can be hooked up to either the lighter or the corvette, and we'll be able to tow it back to R'Bak much faster." She smiled, obviously hoping it would be hers at the end of the mission.

"There's one more point to going there," Bowden said. "If we don't make it, you can hide and refuel. Then, when the corvette goes behind the planet, you can make a low power escape with a long drift back." He shrugged. "At least that way we get the word to them on what happened, and they can prepare for the arrival of the Kulsians." The thought sobered the rest of them, and Bowden hurried on. "Not that that's going to happen, of course, but just as a last resort…"

"Got it," Fiezel said.

"Good," Bowden said as he worked the packet toward the lighter. "It's agreed then. Let's see if our people still control the lighter, or if we're going to have to call our friends upstairs."

"Do you know who they are?" Raptis asked.

"Who? The commandos or the people on the lighter?"

"Either. Both."

"Nope. I would probably know the Terrans if I saw them, but I don't, at this moment, know who they are." *Although I'd bet a lot of money that Harry Tapper is within a kilometer of me right now, one way or the other. That's where I'd want him, anyway.*

Bowden switched to the radio. "New York."

A call came back almost immediately. "Yankees."

"Seriously?" Fiezel asked. "Always hated those guys. I'm more of a Mets fan."

"I didn't pick the code words," Bowden said. "The good news is, though, that our guys are in control of the lighter."

Bowden joined with the lighter and the larger ship extended its boarding tube to them. They connected it to the packet, and Bowden led Hrensku and Raptis over to the lighter. As they reached the hatch, it opened to reveal four men, one of which he knew.

"Welcome," he said to Max Messina. *So this is where he's been hiding.* The big sleepy-eyed bodyguard introduced his compatriots Vat, Chalmers, and Jackson. Bowden recognized them, having seen them on R'Bak a few times, but he wouldn't have expected to see them in control of a spaceship. Jackson looked a lot worse for wear; his head was a mass of bandages.

"Murphy says to tell you great job," Bowden said after he'd introduced Hrensku and Raptis, who'd then gone to check the lighter's navigation and flight station controls. Bowden nodded to the boarding tube. "I guess you'll be leaving now?"

"We talked about that," Chalmers said, "but we're going to stay. We've got too much invested in this op to turn it over completely. We're going to see it to its successful completion."

"Not done yet," Jackson said. He was hard to understand through the bandages. "Going to help out."

Bowden looked at Vat and raised an eyebrow. "I needed a break from the planet," the bunko artist and black-marketeer said with a shrug. "I'm here to the end."

"Besides," Chalmers said, "we've got a wounded Kulsian I don't want to move or make someone else's responsibility. We'll just keep him here, nice and safe." He smiled. "Why don't we get your cargo loaded aboard so you can get rid of that ship before it's seen? We've got too much invested in this to blow it so close to the end."

* * * * *

Chapter Sixteen

"There he goes," Bowden said as the packet moved off to their starboard. Moving the two CONEX boxes into the lighter's hold hadn't been easy, but with the equipment they'd found on the ship—in addition to the assistance provided by Chalmers' team—they'd managed to get them strapped down in a couple of the cargo bays.

After that, they'd sealed off the hold area so the men in the boxes could get out and stretch their legs without the two groups seeing each other. Bowden thought the restriction kind of dumb at this point—if one group got captured, they were all going to get captured—but Murphy had been very clear on keeping the two groups separate. It still didn't make sense to do so, though, as it kept them from coordinating their part of the operation. *Sometimes there are operational imperatives us little guys don't need to know, I guess.*

Chalmers also kept his pet Kulsian—whose name was Yukanna—separate from Bowden's group throughout. *Maybe he thought one of the Dogs would want to kill him.* Bowden shrugged to himself. *There's no reason why—Yukanna is far more valuable alive than dead.*

"Ready?" Raptis asked a little while later once the packet was well clear of them.

"Yeah," Bowden said. "Let's get this started."

Raptis initiated the burn that would put them into orbit.

Bowden looked over his shoulder. "What's the code word for 'we're fat, dumb and happy, and everything is fine?'"

"It's 'Riches,' believe it or not," Chalmers replied.

Bowden chuckled. "Somehow, that makes sense for them." He switched to the radio and pulled out a piece of paper on which he'd written what he wanted to say.

"Why don't I take this," Vat asked, holding out his hand. "I can speak it better than any of you."

Bowden shrugged and handed the transmitter and his script over. "Be my guest."

Vat took a minute to familiarize himself, then he keyed the mic. "Patrol Cycler PH-09, this is *Lighter 03*. Currently entering orbit. Code word: Riches."

When he didn't receive a response, he repeated the transmission.

"*Lighter 03*, Patrol Cycler PH-09. I understand code word: Riches."

"Affirmative, Patrol Cycler PH-09. We are positioned for…wait…shit! *Look out!*"

Bowden reached up, killed the drive, and gave several hard boosts with the ACS system. The ship began tumbling, and the concepts of 'up' and 'down' became lost as his stomach flip-flopped.

Chalmers reached forward and pulled a handle, releasing a batch of simulated accident debris to go along with the first batch he had released prior to Bowden initiating the tumble.

"Collision emergency, PH-09!" Vat continued. "The panel shows multiple small hull breaches, and our attitude control is out. We're…*we're losing atmosphere. Emergency bulkheads not responding. We can't—*" He released the transmit button.

"*Lighter 03*, say again? What was the nature of the collision?"

Bowden smiled.

After a few seconds, Patrol Cycler PH-09 called again. "*Lighter 03*, report your status. Respond immediately. "

Bowden pantomimed dying for a few seconds, until PH-09 called. "If you can hear me, *Lighter 03*, hold on. We are on our way to you. We should be there in approximately three hours."

Bowden took the mic from Vat and attached it to the instrument panel. "Well, we've done our part. Time to wake up the folks in the hold so they can earn their pay." He pressed the button to talk to the commandos. "Bowden calling whoever's in the hold. We're being approached by the Kulsian corvette, ETA three hours. Our part of this mission is over. We got you here. Now...you're up. Go get 'em, boys!"

# # # # #

About Chris Kennedy

A Webster Award winner and three-time Dragon Award finalist, Chris Kennedy is a Science Fiction/Fantasy author, speaker, and small-press publisher who has written over 40 books and published more than 300 others. Get his free book, "Shattered Crucible," at his website, https://chriskennedypublishing.com.

Called "fantastic" and "a great speaker," he has coached hundreds of beginning authors and budding novelists on how to self-publish their stories at a variety of conferences, conventions, and writing guild presentations. He is the author of the award-winning #1 bestseller, "Self-Publishing for Profit: How to Get Your Book Out of Your Head and Into the Stores."

Chris lives in Coinjock, North Carolina, with his wife, and is the holder of a doctorate in educational leadership and master's degrees in both business and public administration. Follow Chris on Facebook at https://www.facebook.com/ckpublishing/.

* * * * *

Find out what's coming from CKP!

Join the Factory Floor and stay in touch!

Meet us at: https://www.facebook.com/groups/461794864654198/

* * * * *

The Caine Riordan Universe

The Caine Riordan series and Terran Republic universe deliver gritty yet doggedly optimistic hard scifi in a world that is a believable and embattled successor to our own. For those who are not familiar with the series' hallmark blend of exploration, alien encounters, intrigue, and action, you can find them all right here:

The **Caine Riordan** series
(Baen Books)
Fire with Fire
Trial by Fire
Raising Caine
Caine's Mutiny
Marque of Caine
Endangered Species (forthcoming)

The **Murphy's Lawless** series
(Beyond Terra Press)
Shakes
Obligations
Man-Eater
Promises
Pearl
Waveoff
Murphy's Lawless

The **Murphy's Lawless: Watch the Skies** series
(Beyond Terra Press)
Sundown
Firefall
Shadows
Murphy's Lawless: Watch the Skies

The **Murphy's Lawless: Mission Critical** series
(Beyond Terra Press)
Infiltration
Insertion
Assault (forthcoming)
Murphy's Lawless: Mission Critical (forthcoming)

Other works in the **Terran Republic** universe
(Beyond Terra Press)
Lost Signals

Since that list includes a winner of the Compton Crook Award, four Nebula finalists, and ten Dragon Award finalists, they're not hard to find. Just go wherever books are sold. Want to learn more about the Caine Riordan series? Easy. Contact any of the publishers, or you can reach out to me at contact@charlesegannon.com.

Want to see more of what's going on in the Terran Republic universe? Check out http://www.charlesegannon.com for exclusive written and visual content.

And if you decide you don't want to miss a single new release or announcement, then go to http://charlesegannon.com/wp/sign-up/ to join the all-inclusive mailing list for sneak peeks, special offers, and features you won't see anywhere else.

And most important of all…welcome aboard; we're glad you're here!

The following is an

Excerpt from Book One of the Revelations Cycle:

Cartwright's Cavaliers

Mark Wandrey

Available Now from Seventh Seal Press

eBook, Paperback, and Audio Book

Excerpt from "Cartwright's Cavaliers:"

The last two operational tanks were trapped on their chosen path. Faced with destroyed vehicles front and back, they cut sideways to the edge of the dry river bed they'd been moving along and found several large boulders to maneuver around that allowed them to present a hull-down defensive position. Their troopers rallied on that position. It was starting to look like they'd dig in when Phoenix 1 screamed over and strafed them with dual streams of railgun rounds. A split second later, Phoenix 2 followed on a parallel path. Jim was just cheering the air attack when he saw it. The sixth damned tank, and it was a heavy.

"I got that last tank," Jim said over the command net.

"Observe and stand by," Murdock said.

"We'll have these in hand shortly," Buddha agreed, his transmission interspersed with the thudding of his CASPer firing its magnet accelerator. "We can be there in a few minutes."

Jim examined his battlespace. The tank was massive. It had to be one of the fusion-powered beasts he'd read about. Which meant shields and energy weapons. It was heading down the same gap the APC had taken, so it was heading toward Second Squad, and fast.

"Shit," he said.

"Jim," Hargrave said, "we're in position. What are you doing?"

"Leading," Jim said as he jumped out from the rock wall.

* * * * *

Get "Cartwright's Cavaliers" now at:
https://www.amazon.com/dp/B01MRZKM95

Find out more about Mark Wandrey and the Four Horsemen Universe at:

https://chriskennedypublishing.com/the-four-horsemen-books/

* * * * *

The following is an

Excerpt from Book One of the Salvage Title Trilogy:

Salvage Title

Kevin Steverson

Available Now from Theogony Books

eBook, Paperback, and Audio Book

Excerpt from "Salvage Title:"

The first thing Clip did was get power to the door and the access panel. Two of his power cells did the trick once he had them wired to the container. He then pulled out his slate and connected it. It lit up, and his fingers flew across it. It took him a few minutes to establish a link, then he programmed it to search for the combination to the access panel.

"Is it from a human ship?" Harmon asked, curious.

"I don't think so, but it doesn't matter; ones and zeros are still ones and zeros when it comes to computers. It's universal. I mean, there are some things you have to know to get other races' computers to run right, but it's not that hard," Clip said.

Harmon shook his head. *Riiigghht,* he thought. He knew better. Clip's intelligence test results were completely off the charts. Clip opted to go to work at Rinto's right after secondary school because there was nothing for him to learn at the colleges and universities on either Tretra or Joth. He could have received academic scholarships for advanced degrees on a number of nearby systems. He could have even gone all the way to Earth and attended the University of Georgia if he wanted. The problem was getting there. The schools would have provided free tuition if he could just have paid to get there.

Secondary school had been rough on Clip. He was a small guy that made excellent grades without trying. It would have been worse if Harmon hadn't let everyone know that Clip was his brother. They lived in the same foster center, so it was mostly true. The first day of school, Harmon had laid down the law—if you messed with Clip, you messed up.

At the age of fourteen, he beat three seniors senseless for attempting to put Clip in a trash container. One of them was a Yalteen, a member of a race of large humanoids from two systems over. It wasn't a fair fight—they should have brought more people with them. Harmon hated bullies.

After the suspension ended, the school's Warball coach came to see him. He started that season as a freshman and worked on using it to earn a scholarship to the academy. By the time he graduated, he was six feet two inches with two hundred and twenty pounds of muscle. He got the scholarship and a shot at going into space. It was the longest time he'd ever spent away from his foster brother, but he couldn't turn it down.

Clip stayed on Joth and went to work for Rinto. He figured it was a job that would get him access to all kinds of technical stuff, servos, motors, and maybe even some alien computers. The first week he was there, he tweaked the equipment and increased the plant's recycled steel production by 12 percent. Rinto was eternally grateful, as it put him solidly into the profit column instead of toeing the line between profit and loss. When Harmon came back to the planet after the academy, Rinto hired him on the spot on Clip's recommendation. After he saw Harmon operate the grappler and got to know him, he was glad he did.

A steady beeping brought Harmon back to the present. Clip's program had succeeded in unlocking the container. "Right on!" Clip exclaimed. He was always using expressions hundreds or more years out of style. "Let's see what we have; I hope this one isn't empty, too." Last month they'd come across a smaller vault, but it had been empty.

Harmon stepped up and wedged his hands into the small opening the door had made when it disengaged the locks. There wasn't enough power in the small cells Clip used to open it any further. He put his weight into it, and the door opened enough for them to get inside. Before they went in, Harmon placed a piece of pipe in the doorway so it couldn't close and lock on them, baking them alive before anyone realized they were missing.

Daylight shone in through the doorway, and they both froze in place; the weapons vault was full.

* * * * *

Get "Salvage Title" now at:
https://www.amazon.com/dp/B07H8Q3HBV.

Find out more about Kevin Steverson and "Salvage Title" at:
http://chriskennedypublishing.com/.

* * * * *

Made in United States
Orlando, FL
16 January 2022

13529723R00085